PLASMAS

Céline Minard

PLASMAS

Translated by Annabel L. Kim

DEEP VELLUM PUBLISHING
DALLAS, TEXAS

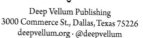

Deep Vellum Publishing
3000 Commerce St., Dallas, Texas 75226
deepvellum.org · @deepvellum

Deep Vellum is a 501c3 nonprofit literary arts organization
founded in 2013 with the mission to bring
the world into conversation through literature.

Support for this publication has been provided in part by the National
Endowment for the Arts, the Texas Commission on the Arts, the City of
Dallas Office of Arts and Culture, the Communities Foundation of Texas, and
the Addy Foundation.

ISBNs: 978-1-64605-352-0 (paperback) | 978-1-64605-364-3 (ebook)

LIBRARY OF CONGRESS CATALOGING-IN-PUBLICATION DATA

Names: Minard, Céline, author. | Kim, Annabel L., translator.
Title: Plasmas / Céline Minard ; translated by Annabel L. Kim.
Other titles: Plasmas. English
Description: First US edition. | Dallas, Texas : Deep Vellum Publishing,
2024.
Identifiers: LCCN 2024008920 (print) | LCCN 2024008921 (ebook) | ISBN
9781646053520 (trade paperback) | ISBN 9781646053643 (ebook)
Subjects: LCGFT: Novels.
Classification: LCC PQ2713.I53 P5313 2024 (print) | LCC PQ2713.I53
(ebook) | DDC 843/.92--dc23/eng/20240301
LC record available at https://lccn.loc.gov/2024008920
LC ebook record available at https://lccn.loc.gov/2024008921

Cover Design by Vic Peña
Interior Layout and Typesetting by KGT

Brigham, this is stupid stuff!
Tell us a story, old man,
or old woman as the case may be,
or old Tiresias, chirping like a cricket,
tell us a story with a proper end to it
instead of beginning again and again like this
and thereby achieving a muddle
which is not by nature after anything in particular
nor does it have anything consequent to it
but it just hangs there
placidly eating its tail.

Ursula K. Le Guin
Dancing at the Edge of the World

CONTENTS

In the Air

The room is buzzing with electricity. They're all there, waiting in the dark, cameras on standby, sensors turned off, idle since they took their places in order, one by one, silent and stock still.

Galván is standing on the starting board, warmed up, stretched out, trembling, he's waiting for the ray of light that will launch him into action. He knows how to spend the twenty seconds from spotlight to takeoff. Eyes closed, he's concentrating on the gradual disappearance of the phosphene provoked by the spotlight that will take hold of him and not let go during the thirty-five minutes to come. If everything goes well.

Rodric is in the middle of climbing below opposite him, he hears him. Lena will join him in a few seconds in the spotlight. She will lean on his shoulder to seize the bar. All three of them will then sense the singular click of three thousand reactivated sensors.

Galván breathes carefully, he's counting. His sweat is beginning to soak his bodysuit at the armpits, at the hollows of his knees and of his lower back. The cloth swells imperceptibly, the ventilation is kicking in. He misses his old graphene leotard, which would stink well before the end of his warmup. But no human is authorized to move any more without being connected to their electro-organic girdle. They're processing all the data, all the time. And it isn't right now, not tonight, that he's going to escape from it.

The three thousand Bjorgs occupying the orchestra pit have come for that—to collect, analyze, and transform data. In real time and in reconstituted real conditions.

The rigs are dated: the apron is spread out twelve meters below the boards, four above the sawdust and sand strewn across the track—you'd think you were actually at the real thing. The rows have been adapted. No longer seats, but ramps made of pliable resin spiraling into a gentle slope around the central circle, which they've rolled onto to climb up to their respective turnouts. The differences in reception will be negligible.

Mechanical observation is no longer the point. Galván knows the Bjorgs' long history toward fluidity of movement. The eagerness of humans then of modulars to equal the agility of organisms. Human records were pulverized a long time ago. In every discipline. They jump, swim, fly, throw higher, farther, deeper, they hit harder, they run faster. On blades of soft steel, the Bjorgs, minimally equipped, act as lures in greyhound races. With the requisite presets to keep the dogs out of breath and lead them faster, always faster, toward their end. They went through thousands of them before reducing the critical threshold zone to a single point. Precise, unbeatable. The Bjorgs' analysis is efficient.

The rope ladder oscillates against the metal of the crossbar. Lena climbs up as if weightless, she flows up from inside the hemp braid that holds her up, she passes from one level to the next without pausing, goes past the board and lands on it. She touches Galván on the shoulder, the projector floods them with light. She grabs the bar, keeping it in her hand, heating it up. Galván has his eyes closed. Rodric is on the trapeze in front of them, sitting, moving. His forearms are white, powdered to the elbows. His grips shine with a matte luster. He swings, balancing on one buttock and the end of a thigh, his legs dangling. The luminous ghost has faded underneath Galván's eyelids, Rodric is hanging by the backs of his knees; shoulders and head relaxed, he takes on speed with each go, each return. It's a moment he relishes. The progressive inversion of his body's orientation. This minute of setting up, of reuniting with his posture, the anchoring in his thighs, the presence of his skull, the pins and needles in his fingers. He takes advantage, he is at home, solid, a catcher.

And Galván suddenly holds the bar in both hands. Makes his little starting leap, legs tense, pointed, and takes off. No fanfare, the only sounds will be those of the rig, bodies, breaths, impacts, and wind whistling in his ears from the first travel. Arms tense, braced, legs squared at the return, he increases in strength, grows light and heavy in equal measure, takes the pressure, summons it, revokes it, and runs through his trick. A perilous double leap at the end of which Rodric says to him, "Give!", and he gives—his hands, his life, his heart—in the same movement. One single look exchanged between them and Galván executes his return in one and a half pirouettes. Sweeping, slow, a fulgurant promenade. Ten seconds of life in all and for all. The board vibrates under the authority of his weight, found again. He is there, in his element, in full possession of his faculties, lucid, sharp, he thinks only of leaving it again. But Lena has fled with the trapeze, he must wait for her. She goes back up for the second travel, begins her descent; the point of each foot at either end of the bar, she reaches the apogee, lets go, plunges, vertical, legs closed, arms taut, palms joined, and offers her ankles to Rodric, who takes them.

He holds her, his head at the bottom, full of water, full of blood, he feels his resistance descend into the legs of Lena, who grazes the air with her fingers and seems to draw it, tear it apart, he holds her to throw her again, to transmit to her in momentum what she gave him in the impact that launched both of them toward the back, toward the front, he throws her, the bar cuts into his tibias,

Galván has sent back the baton, Lena tops him, pirouettes, and seizes the return as he passes. Her hands are enormous. All veins visible. She does not smile as she reaches the board. She never had to. This is not a show. This is not one species examining another—then takes off again, wild. The only ones who know what they're doing, that evening, are the three of them.

The unladen trapeze makes six movements while Rodric opens the bag of chalk hooked onto his belt, plunges in his right hand, closes it, and lets a trail of powder form on the stretch of the curve he's crossing, his ambitus, his territory.

The Bjorgs are hermetic, insensible to the fine particles.

Galván is there to turn the triple as it's been done for centuries, since antiquity. His technique is irreproachable, it's broken-in. The Bjorgs, who master the quintuple and the sextuple, aren't done, however, with him, with his art, with, perhaps, his fear. The variations in his levels of adrenaline: sky-rocketing at the very beginning of his start, going down during the travel, settling into the trick— more stable than a center of gravity as he's turning round on himself as around a fixed axis—ticking up at the moment of meeting, just before hearing the catcher, feeling him, seeing him at last, his eyes like two inverted lakes gorged with life, with held back tears.

They aren't done with Rodric either. With what connects them across the void, what escapes their measurements. The calculations of forces, fluid mechanics, chemistry.

He turns and returns. Rodric hits into his hands. Lena takes off again.

She launches off the board with a dry, very confined leap—the only effort she appears to put forth herself, drawing from her body, from her personal strength, the sole act where her will manifests, decisive and collected like a bullet. The movement after which everything is said and done even though nothing has yet played out, taken place, taken form except in her flesh and already in the air that carries her. She's gone past the trick she will carry out. Concerned solely with her suspension, palms closed around the bar, still in the movement of the rig, in the mass of gas that surrounds her. It isn't she who moves, but the elements around her. The bar, the catcher, the apron, the crossbar. She lets go of them in all directions, she makes them spin, takes hold of them again as they fall, repositions them, sends them flying again, drives them mad, then comes back, the bar in her hands, the board under her feet, gravity in the earth, air in her mouth.

Lena is not an aerialist, she couldn't care less about falling.

The Bjorgs cannot manage to quantify her level of absence.

Galván is in place for the quadruple. He breathes in and out as he jumps. Galvan's always the same, a rope, an assemblage of sticks and elastic bands, a state of mind tempered like steel, a hard arrow that will become a top and send itself into space, out of reach, out of range, intransigent. It's this momentum that sends him flying. The second, the tenth of a second where the movement starts off and invades him, tows him, takes him as if he were a wave in the ocean, elementary force, contact. An eternity, much shorter than any length of time. After which Rodric's arms return his body to him, Rodric's eyes confirm his flight, and the bar his weight.

The Bjorgs constantly recalculate his density.

They are looking for a flaw. If it doesn't show up, they will provoke it.

Lena clambers onto Galván's shoulders. Perched, she performs the quadruple from another vantage point. He holds the trapeze within her reach above his head, waiting to feel her grip next to his before letting go, bracing himself for the recoil that her absence will inflict on him. A featherweight that takes off like a loaded gun. She has jumped. Galván vibrates with the steel ropes he's holding onto. Lena is launched. She opens her legs at the end of the travel to accelerate the first descent, rises very high, very far above him, square to the peak of her course, her feet brushing up against her hands beneath the bar, then, in slow motion, she begins her second descent, sitting in the air, unfolding little by little, suddenly upright, sucked up by the ascent, she picks up speed. At the highest point of her curve, before the energy is canceled and inverted, she opens her fingers and begins. The first revolution of the jump could be anyone's, it shows up in the world balled up like a fist, the lungs are compressed, greedy, clogged, as certain as the instinct of an ancient species; the following one breathes and passes from life to life as it changes form, the knees spread apart; the third one accelerates, going through walls, sound, light; Lena winds the fourth one up on the swing of her human childhood before leaping into the inside of the fall itself, settling into it, letting herself float, fall, feeling her arms rise, take off, hold on to and disintegrate the power inside Rodric's shoulders. Then, she's sorry that he, the catcher, is there, tenacious. That he doesn't let her do one round after another, fall after fall, pursue her trajectory and finally initiate the course. Above ground, rid of fulcra, of the dynamic, the envelope, the braided girdle through which the movement, which has just fled, took place. Uncatchable.

The Bjorgs look for the flaw without seeing it.

She looks at Rodric, the brightness, the dark irises, the long lashes, she smiles, she's going to take off again.

Two pirouettes wait for her in the middle of the path, two and a half pirouettes. The flaw, somewhere, and the unmoving Bjorgs.

Snow Globes

They're heavy. Cool in the hand. They're the last three, placed on shelf XVIII of the Conservatory's manudigitals display. The last three in the world. Their weight doesn't vary but their temperature rises when one touches them for long enough. By two or three degrees, just enough to feel the difference. This heating up doesn't have anything to do with the chosen scenario, but nobody can prevent themselves from establishing a correlation between what's happening inside the heart of the sphere and the sensation that spreads through the hollow of the palm. The mushrooms that explode to the point of crushing their plume and vaporous cuticle against the semi-liquid glass wall are, however, not always ochre or red. But if a cloud of milk warms a cup of tea, an atomic flash warms the earth. It's an inherited thought, epigenetic, involuntary. It's also a fact. And the representation of facts, when it reaches the miniature precision attained by the generation capable of producing manudigitals of this quality, produces effects.

The first time Helen held the mobile glass ball, as large as a cultivated apple, in her hand, she had made an awkward movement during the ignition phase. A kind of instinctive jolt upon seeing one half of the sphere, the Earth, light up all of a sudden, upon recognizing Africa bathed in blue water and white light. What had surprised her wasn't the form of the continent, or its harsh lighting, but the presence of the dark vein of the Nile and the surface of Cairo, a very visible gingko leaf at the edge of the desert. Seven minutes after the start of the animation, she had watched the river shrink, fade, bury itself in the drab ochre of the sand, and the city get swallowed up. On the dark side of the marble, through clouds, she made out the electric constellation of America, the appendix of Florida, the brilliant craters of New York, Philadelphia, Baltimore, Atlanta, the black holes of the great lakes punched out of the shining cloth of Chicago, Detroit, Toronto, and Ottawa.

From Houston to Minneapolis, the network was clear, organized in quadrilaterals, strewn with sumptuous, sometimes free-flowing expanses, looser in the Rocky Mountains, then suddenly Los Angeles and San Francisco stretched out on the edge of the abyss, stuck to the side, gilded in fine gold.

At sea, in a straight line and orthogonally, hundreds of fishing boats impossible to make out were piling up in their respective radii, stuck in territorial waters, lined up, set down, crammed together against imaginary boundaries, lying in wait for their prey. Blown up at the start of the animation, wiped out with the first coastal cities. Just a few minutes after large icy petals, under the flowing cotton of suspended water, had detached themselves from the polar marble, immediately embarking on a rapid drift, diminishing soon thereafter, dividing into myriad heralds of spring, the time of flowers. Helen had noticed from her first viewing the fascinating lightness of these displacements and how obvious their sequence was. The ice pollen, spread out and scattered around the oceans, had freed pale lands bristling with volcanic stalks rushing to bloom. The gray smoke rose up powerfully, brought out by red, crowned with ashes, rivers of black mud cracking and sliding down the slopes, revealing molten rock, stamens of fire, which caught the water with a whistle, launching long peduncles of gas raked by winds. Volcanic flowers then opened wherever the seeds had been hidden, coming up out of the earth, the water, the hollows of caverns and from the depths of the faults. In broad daylight, Siberia lit up, the Amazon sparkled, California was ablaze. Petroleum flares caught fire in the middle of the desert, entire reserves were burning to deliver up black corollas of fossil oils. The browns and pinks of burning vegetation were growing into large plumes—snatched up, swept up, rolled into the dance of cyclones at the hot center. They traversed the Atlantic, brushing past land, instigating a sequence of whirling figures and evolutions, slipping their arum skin full of salt into the volume secured between water and glass. Whole bouquetfuls.

And the season passed. The center of the sphere disappeared for a moment under a homogenous aerosol flecked with specks. Then what was being held was a ball of smoke as fragile as a soap bubble and just as empty.

The dust from the bloom fell. It settled slowly, landing on still surfaces, emphasizing hills, carpeting the plains, marking liquids. Everything was gray, black, covered in a layer of thick powder, a carpet of irregular fractals mixed with brown, streaked with white. The winds blew away and recomposed the earth. The tides mixed rock and ash with sand. The embers choked in the night zone until they were extinguished entirely. The clouds lost mass and reformed, lighter, washing the earth from the tops of the peaks. Mountains slid down, the great rivers stirred, taking on volume, driving the alluvia and forcing the dams to rejoin the seas. The salty flows became brighter. And green appeared. As dots, then as larger and larger stains covering the newly emerged lands in their entirety. It occupied the eastern coast of North America, tracing, through capillarity, the old network of lights to the center of the continent, it held the rivers in their courses, running on plateaus, leaping up slopes. Eurasia was covered with an uninterrupted light coat in its northern part, Australia was tucking itself in, Africa was finding its heart again, South America, its headdress, dress, and jewelry. And the cyclones continued to brew, the oceans, to brighten and swallow up islands and borders.

When sand emerged from the foam on the coastline, forming the line of a blond contour, when lagunas appeared in the Caspian Sea, mangroves at the tip of Somalia, coral reefs in Australia, Helen would stop the animation. Everyone knew what came next. Her audience couldn't handle any mention of the series of events that had taken place in this late-stage Antiquity. Lassitude, more rarely anger, made them deaf to this historical period.

She would put the sphere back on shelf XVIII of the display and suggest to two of her students (female, preferably) that they light up the other two manudigitals simultaneously. The pale Moon and dusty Mars. The hypotheses of that era.

They would then see the satellite and the red planet come alive, a miniscule life constrained to a few craters. First, on the Moon, with structures for life, drilling, and quick assembly, then on Mars a few minutes later. Nuclear reactors, solar panels, water and oxygen bubbles, greenhouses, the entry to habitation tunnels, the park where Rovers and Voltigers would soon cover hundreds of acres. The data from this period of so-called settlement were still available. As well as a dozen exploration narratives that Helen was fond of for their enthusiasm and awkwardness. No human at the time could hold back their emotion in the face of the Valles Marineris, a rift nine times deeper than the Grand Canyon.

Mars had a small circumference, but it was dramatic, excessive, and fundamentally hostile to any aerobic form of life. The men sent first were engineers, researchers, and scientists in peak physical condition, not very inclined to passive contemplation. They had provided data, descriptions of experiments and more or less provisory conclusions. But the second wave of colonization was more heterogeneous. It was this wave that had produced the imprecise narratives that Helen valued so much and that she had been trying, for two decades, to teach to these young people who had never seen the Earth, Moon, or Mars except in cognitive material. How do you make someone who has never walked in an environment subjected to a gravitational force understand that climbing up a slope was an effort that no Earthling would have been surprised to have to make. How do you make them feel the confusion of the amateur alpinist finding themselves at the edge of the Ulysses Tholus volcano, content with their feat and their all-encompassing view of the landscape, but terribly frustrated by being stuck in a suit without which they could not maintain their vital functions. How do you transmit the paradoxical sensation that they experienced so intimately—in flesh and in knowledge. Of being there, alive, at the peak of their strength, lifted up by endorphins, in an environment they had just roamed around in, which would kill them in fifteen seconds if they gave in to the impulse to lift up their visor to take a simple breath. Someone for whom the outside was always both unbreathable and uncrossable shouldn't give in to any nostalgia for an open, welcoming space. Unless this idea was itself inherited, the way Eden had been for some, Nature, for others. Earth, for the exiles.

Each time Helen read Abaigh Dixon's great poem out loud, the audience sighed. The last verses riled up even the most reserved and recalcitrant listeners in systematic fashion. No one there, however, had felt on their skin the earthly wind recollected by the Martian poet who, carried away, used an infinite number of contrasting variations to move it through her verses with tenderness as if it were passing through a net. Maybe they understood better than Helen what this emptiness was made of, this dynamic absence that circulated between words, stones, against the grass, and in waves and undone hair. But a sunrise? Or the appearance of Phobos and Deimos in the dark night from behind the translucent wall of a tiny Martian shelter? What could they find moving about these things? For these interstellar nomads, born in space, detached from everything, the idea of a life punctuated by the appearance of a star and a satellite was surely marvelously archaic. Helen was unmoved because she hadn't experienced these things—what she remembered was the smell of humus, dogs, cats, the color of shells and the taste of buds. While she was in a position to share, as an equal, the feeling of loss that Abaigh Dixon was delivering up, she couldn't perceive Mars's two moons as anything other than a screen onto which the author projected the ectoplasm of another world—lost. Which was what the two worlds were from the beginning for her students. They dug deeper into the memory of their species and Helen wasn't far from thinking that they had access to a hidden meaning, swallowed up in the core of the Earth, which she could not attain, precisely because she had known it close up and was limited to a personal experience that hadn't been transmitted, but lived.

In the Martian globe that Erenborg held as if it were treasure, little whirlwinds of dust were chasing each other against the backdrop of what had been Mars's ocean. They traversed this territory—Arcadia, Utopia, the Elysium of Exiles—following erratic trajectories whose direction reversed suddenly at the outskirts of the ancient coastline. When they crossed the rocky bulge, they crumbled in a few seconds. The others grew larger as they raked the bottom of the powdery plateau, swallowing each other up to split up even more and drop, inert, into little pointy piles that a cutting wind dispersed onto the surface as if to put them back into play. The dust devils' high-speed chase never stopped. Sometimes, a bigger tornado passed, absorbing all the others and falling apart against a mountain, leaving behind, for a few moments, a perfectly flat and empty terrain. But the little devils reformed here and there, remaking their teams and taking their ambulatory activities back up. It was a show that was as fascinating as that of the wake a boat leaves behind, opening and closing endlessly. This phenomenon—no one could explain why it was concentrated in the place where the Boreal Ocean had disappeared—had damaged the electrical installations of the first Positions. To such an extent that the land-use plan had quickly been revised by the campists and the generators moved to shelter at the Arsia and Pavonis foothills. An engineer from the second wave had devoted his time to running after these devils. Equipped with cameras, weighed down with measuring instruments, he entered the whirlwinds and attempted to follow their course from the inside, to stay inside the center of the column no matter how quickly it was moving, to capture its molecular structure, the variations induced by the augmentation of its mass, and to determine the cause of their disintegration.

His work had been classified as "artistic with deferred results." Helen had found entire pages dedicated to the description of the moment he crossed the wall of dust and found himself inside the vacuum tube of the climatic entity. Surrounded by particles in continuous circular motion, sometimes so close he couldn't hold out his hand without modifying the circuit, deafened by the sound of friction, disoriented by the lack of bearings, it nonetheless systematically evoked a state of internal peace. Which was all the more intense for being transitory. He didn't feel threatened but protected, removed from a part of the world that oppressed him.

Erenborg held the Mars manudigital in her left hand, her arm stretched out before her so that everyone could see what was happening inside. Her yellow eyes fixed on the artifact with the intensity of a magnetic field. She just glanced over from time to time at the white globe of the Moon that Borgen, just as focused as she was, was brandishing. But the climatic and geological activity there remained so discreet that it wasn't really much of a show. The helium-3 mines were spreading on the ground like oil stains, the mega-factories producing Starshot probes took up the entirety of the Ptolemaeus Crater but they didn't change much and the electromagnetic turbulence generated by the interaction between the Moon and the Sun wasn't as lively as the Mars devils.

The cold light of the earthling satellite was an extinguished halo to which only Helen gave a somewhat old-fashioned poetic connotation. The grand narratives that had established it as a possible world were full of verbal inventions and science, but the Moon had been too exploited, and with an urgency too intense, for it to remain something to dream about. There wasn't anything free about the sidestep that humanity had had to make after the lights went out. Exile isn't a choice. In the best case, it is an alternative to immediate death.

The highlight of the lunar manudigital's animation was thousands of solar sails taking off with their probes loaded, propelled by blinding laserflashes. There was so much equipment for exploration being launched in such a large quantity that it looked like a plague of locusts, a cloud of insects held up and driven forward by a rain of piercing red lines. The takeoff was massive, recurrent, stroboscopic, and the probes reached twenty percent of the speed of light in the blink of an eye, the solar sails shone violently and disappeared immediately upon contact with the semi-liquid glass whose volume comprised merely the equivalent of an atmosphere four hundred kilometers thick. The escape to Alpha Centauri was a matter of two blinks of an eye. And a journey of four point five light years during which the Moon returned to its icy pallor, to the orbit and decorative phases that no human eye would see anymore from Earth.

Her students had been born in the vessel of the Grand Departure, they watched with meticulous interest what was for them the beginning of their history. The only human adventure still taking place.

The Starshot probes had taken ten years to transmit the information that the Navigators were waiting for in order to determine their course. Ten short years during which the assembly of the vessel had been finalized through desperate efforts. The lunar factories had provided the incredible mass of helium that the plasma engines required, leaving both the subsoil and men drained. On Mars, the third period had begun, marked by increasingly violent storms and electrical problems that had reached a critical mass. Which you couldn't see in the manudigital's animation because it had been conceived before the collapses, with the goal of drawing the necessary workforce to Mars and the Moon while Earth was choking on itself and reacting with increasing violence to the attempts at readjustment that were being instated. As the Embarkees had established as a matter of fact, the space probes launch was the last chance for the survival of the species.

During the previous riots, at the center of Europe where survivors had gathered, numerous scenes of savage violence and desolation had been seen. Helen wasn't a supporter of this direct method. She would not show the testimonial films that, according to her, only transmitted fear, horror, and the visceral hatred living beings had for themselves. Like all genocide archives. But she always showed, at the end of the bachelor's degree, a short film on a reel which followed a group of children and adolescents left to themselves in the ruins of a building in Oxford.

They were dirty, thin, merry as the camera rolled because they had just discovered a box full of intact cans of food and a case of terrestrial manudigitals. They could be seen throwing up the metal cylinders with a ferocious and impressive joy. They could be seen running, overflowing with life, famished, impetuous. They could be seen devouring the contents of the cans while they were still inside the boxes that had been cut open with a knife, licking the sharp-edged lids; they could be seen fighting each other for a falling morsel. Then, all of a sudden, they could be seen playing.

The toppled-over box of manudigitals had let out dozens of spheres that rolled about on the floor, spinning round and round, scattering through the room. These lit their feet with a cold light. They kicked them to the center of the circle the group formed, they sent them back at each other more and more quickly, and the movements that had been disordered at first became orderly, settling down, responding to each other. They could be seen smiling when the dance of the spheres and the feet reached the virtuosity of starlings flying and changing direction in one fluid, concerted instant.

Helen's students also smiled at that moment.

Then a hand broke free of a body, plunged into the mass, grabbed a sphere and without anything slowing down, the young man threw a sparkling Earth into the air, with all his strength.

They all looked at it.

They all looked at the ascending arc—invisible, inexorable—on which it had embarked. Their expressions hadn't yet had time to change, they had already understood, the game was already over. The film stopped before the sphere reached the apogee of its trajectory.

Tar Pits

The bubble formed slowly on the lake's surface. Heavy from all the eddies that had let it
pass through ancient obstacles, finally liquified. Flexible, thick like a skin, lush like a plant, it
swelled in the middle of the bottomless puddle,
which hid its cards under an inch of clear water.
Methane dilated its sides with the savoir-faire of
a master glassblower. Out of a blister, it made a
dome, flawless geometry coated in a shimmer-
ing substance. It heated it up and carried it to the
threshold of formal perfection, to the point where
it might well close in on itself, form a complete
sphere, and free itself from the material that had
witnessed its birth. But the bubble always burst
before detaching from the plane.

During their long death throes, the ones who
had drowned in this lake had had limitless time to

let themselves be distracted by the recurring spectacle of these tar buds filled up with gas. Appearing, developing, tissues steadily increasing in tension, uprising, desiring to escape, gathering momentum, exploding—all this must have been a comforting sight for these bodies, stuck and consigned to an unbearable weight. The raptors, in particular, latched onto the flanks and backs of their prey, perched on their skulls, their talons driven in then stuck with asphaltite to bloody eye sockets, must have enjoyed all the details. Observing over and over the absolute velocity of the bubbles' disappearance. They had been able to watch them open directly onto the void, one by one or all at once, like a carpet of aborted germinations.

Hagop imagined them yanking their necks toward the sky as if they wanted to rip them off, feathers stuck together, wings leaden, feet already fossilized. He wondered if they cursed the wooly mammoth, mastodon, and wolf who had ventured to drink this deceptive water that swallowed them up slowly, or if they cursed themselves and thought of themselves as belonging with the imbeciles.

Hagop Bates had been seated for five hours,

bent over the eyepiece of his optical microscope, he had hardly changed position and was beginning to feel his neck get stiff. He was completely absorbed in removing the beetle shell from what coated it. It was a warm color, browned like old leather, soft despite the harsh light that lit up his work surface, and he thought he felt its delicate texture under his dental tools as if he were touching it with the pad of his finger. He had been getting close for three days. He had first sensed its form in the little black ball that had been left on his lab bench. Then, little by little, he had figured out its contours by feeling around inside of the matter, progressing by way of little touches, identifying points of weakness, insinuating the tip of his microhammer into them to deliver the decisive thrust—hundreds of times. He went around the general form, his movements indiscernible, little shavings leaping away from the shapeless mass. He worked like an insect circling another insect, his strategy that of a nuptial dance, coming together and drawing apart unpredictably. His curettes touched down and retracted like antennae, feeling the engulfed body through its sedimentary envelope and bringing it back to life, to the present moment, to its structure and nuance.

A Pleistocene beetle is as shiny as a Holocene beetle but, lacquered as it is by thousands of centuries, it's more energetic and vibrant. Its shell has made good on its promises, it's intact, infused with time. And Hagop was working to allow it to remain so. He was touching only the emptiness that encircled it, slicing only the adhesions. To finish, he sandblasted the patina, taking care not to break through it by even a micrometer. The fossil's most fragile dimension was its having lasted so long, it's what gave it its value and made it immeasurably more precious in his eyes than a living beetle. His meticulous work was much appreciated by the paleontologists who had hired him. Hagop could unset an ammonite as easily as he could the wing of a dipteron, he could prepare an impeccably polished lamina thirty thousandths of a millimeter in thickness, he mastered the microprobes and was authorized to make all kinds of calibrations on the scanning electron microscopes. You could even ask him to clean up his workspace before leaving. He was a laboratory technician without equal.

You couldn't, on the other hand, borrow his tools or point out to him that he ground his teeth while working.

Those who had bought him a drink on Wilshire Boulevard at the end of the workday had seen themselves get too carried away for their tastes to want to repeat the experience. Hagop Bates had his pet theories. He was convinced that he entered into a time capsule every morning that he then left each evening at exactly 6:00 PM to rediscover a world that was neither more nor less coeval with him, but far louder.

All day, in extremely precarious acrobatic conditions, Hagop did battle in the middle of the Ice Age. He carried out excavations in the presence of great predators and unknown pollens and bacteria. He performed for ten to twelve hours a day in a changing environment where the smallest unjustified displacement was a fatal error. He pushed forward into the heart of the trap and knew it. The La Brea tar pits were the black heart of Los Angeles. Los Angeles was the exoskeleton of the subterranean creature whose heartbeat regularly came up and overflowed, from Hancock Park to the intersection of Wilshire and Curson Avenue. When that happened, the fire department was called, they spread entire tankers' worth of cement aggregate on the roadway, absorbing the excess material—the crisis passed and everything went back to normal. Hagop knew that this was merely the manifestation of an extrasystole, perhaps of psychical origins, maybe linked to activity further off on the coast, in Long Beach, Venice, or the oil fields of Inglewood, near Culver City. There were multiple possible explanations.

Hagop wasn't an alcoholic. He stopped himself after the second drink and if his interlocutor insisted on a third, he generally ordered a sugar-free Coke. He was vegan because living surrounded by predation had put him off of dead flesh. Because of its appearance, barbecue sauce gave him nausea, even on tofu. In a pinch, he could swallow fresh oysters and pretend to be a great telluric animal, but he wasn't crazy, he didn't believe it. Hagop had a keen sense of moderation. It's for this reason, undoubtedly, that when Baran Blizzard came and offered ten thousand dollars for an assessment, he immediately grew defensive. There were plenty of nutcase potheads on the beaches, but they didn't pay anybody ten thousand dollars to go digging around in their gardens.

Baran Blizzard, however, was convincing. He knew how to listen. He knew how to make a suggestion without overstepping and, despite his looking like a still muscular hippie, he displayed a certain rigor of thought and a solid knowledge of geology. Contrary to what Hagop had suspected, Baran wasn't a retired Silicon Valley engineer but a former oil prospector and a writer in his spare time, whose *Oil Notes* had been well received in its day. He lived on Sawtelle Boulevard, just above a fault that cut through his garden and divided his house into two uneven parts. He had installed a multi-gas detector at the spot where the floor of his garage had split. He measured the concentrations of radon and hydrogen sulfide every morning before leaving to go on a jog. He could provide the numbers if they were of use. Some nights, the polished concrete shone underneath the tires of his Tesla, enough to light up the chassis. He had gotten used to this glow and spent several minutes each evening looking at it after his meditation session.

Baran Blizzard loved the La Brea Tar Pits Museum. He came regularly to stroll through it. His only regret was that dogs weren't allowed and so he couldn't show his schnauzer, Beebee, the skulls of dangerous wolves lining the orange room's wall. Monsters.

Blending in with the occasional visitors, he had observed Hagop several times behind the lab windows. The blue gloves, the immaculate clusters of cotton swabs in their transparent compartments, the tweezers that separated the wheat from the chaff, and, most of all, his movements. Items requiring the use of a microhammer were rare at La Brea, the fossils extracted from the pits were covered in a soft, viscous coating and technicians usually turned to solvents rather than to mechanical methods. Baran had already noticed the almost sensual tenderness Hagop displayed when he ran the small cotton ball over the length of a femur, but, when he witnessed the slow combat that he engaged in, deploying a simple dental explorer against a tiny black pearl lodged between a mole's metacarpals, he understood whom he was dealing with. Hagop was as methodical and strained as a dung beetle working away. He had never once lifted his eyes from his work before extracting the pellet and leaving a perfectly clean mole paw on his plate. Copper, gold, warm like all the La Brea fossils, but absolutely smooth.

The color of the bones that emerged from the tar trap was so particular and agreeable to look at that Baran had, for a long time, adhered to the theory that it was a ritual burial ground. The skeletons that were removed from it were more beautiful than a work of art. Cleaned, stripped of flesh, organs, tendons, and dregs, they radiated a contained light powerful enough to be seen with the naked eye. The four thousand mammoths, six hundred wolves, hundreds of saber-toothed tigers, dragonflies, toads, mice, and thousands of bugs that had sunk into this hole couldn't have dreamt of a better conserved or more elegant postmortem body. They constituted a population with its own ecosystem, food chain, and all the rest. A world. Who knows, maybe for the animals the La Brea lakes were the portal to Valhalla, to hell, Eden, or eternal life. After all, several species had never come back from there. There were perhaps caves lined with warm lichens, lakes, oceans close to the earth's core. A different, lighter form of life. Hagop shook his head while listening, he'd heard it all before. And the former prospector wasn't wrong, it was indeed an entire world, including climatic variations. But he was mistaken in thinking that it was lost. There were certainly ways of getting inside, you had to be capable of certain mindsets, but the Pleistocene was there, right under their feet, not somewhere else, not past. So, when Baran confided to him that he had a fossil from the future in his garage, rising through layers buried so deeply that they were from a time yet to come, because the world doesn't spin around just one axis but several, he made the decision to take on the assessment.

It wasn't the house of a millionaire, but Baran Blizzard, his car, and his dog lived comfortably. Hagop went on a tour of the fissures in the living room, bathroom, and closet. He attentively noted the one that was snaking its way through the garden and went on to disappear under the jacuzzi. He waited for nightfall to observe the luminescence of the garage. And he concluded that beginning

45

a shallow dig wouldn't be unfounded. The uppermost layer situated underneath the mortar was, in effect, unusual. Its sediments merited analysis and the long form that showed up about 110 centimeters beneath the soil level was unexpected enough to make him want to examine it. For Hagop, the La Brea tar pits were a huge puzzle. A memory shattered, but whole, with all its pieces, which it was merely a question of putting back together. The only limits this place had were human, those of rigor and patience. Everything was there, perfectly conserved—in a state of disorder and all mixed up, but there. Nothing missing, no lacuna, no loss that could disrupt the aggregate. Not a single blade of grass was missing from the prairie that had been swallowed up by them, not a single pollen exine. In Baran's garage, on the other hand, the situation was much more unstable. The neighborhood between Westwood and Sawtelle was positioned both above a fault and a liquefaction zone that extended to the ocean to the south and to Beverly Hills to the north. His house was suspended above a chasm and held up by terrain that was ready to give out with the slightest stress. It was inevitable that the basement had been tossed about multiple times over the course of the last ten thousand years. The leaks must have been substantial. The deposits as well.

This chaotic position ought to have put Hagop off, but Baran had piqued his curiosity, and the almost greenish light that lit up the garage was captivating. It transformed the room's atmosphere. At the edge of the microfault, he had the feeling of being perched on a ghost tree's secondary branch, himself part of an evanescent, but visible canopy, more perceptible than a hologram. Was he a bird still hovering, head tilted, fascinated by the prey that was going to get away from him or to trap him 110 centimeters below? Would he be lost the moment that his feet left their perch, that his wings opened, or would he fall like a ball, his flight feathers tightly packed, hunched toward his prey, his beak as heavy as a nutcracker? Was he still a litho-preparer at the Museum of Natural History, competent and meticulous, or was he something else entirely? In Baran's garage, the world was opening onto multiple yawning gaps at once. And it was rather exciting.

The upper layer had clearly been inconsistent. The long form that had driven Baran to hire Hagop was dissimilar to the layer of sediment from which it had been taken—it was an enclosed rock whose composition demonstrated, despite the principle of cross-checking, that it was more recent than the sediments containing it. Which wasn't exactly possible, even with the hypothesis of a synformal anticline that might have built up there during a tectonic episode that was more violent than the rest.

Hagop had decided to grab the bull by the horns. He made a list of tools that was as long as his arm, which he'd given to Baran before going back home to grab two or three of his favorite tools and his mud gear. In three days, they had opened up the microfault enough to be able to slide in up to the neck and begin the extraction in relative comfort.

The object was bigger than expected. Hagop dug horizontally above the protuberance that had drawn their attention. He had dug up several cubic meters of soil without, for all that, being able to see the form's shape in its entirety. He hoped not to have to prop up the tunnel that was beginning to form, all while calculating, as a precaution, the size and number of beams he would need should that turn out to be necessary.

Baran was a tremendous help. Stripped to the waist, in shorts and work boots, he hauled rubble away discreetly in a wheelbarrow to the dumpster he'd had set up in front of his place. He had the consistency of a good worker, sweating without complaining, pacing himself and stopping only when Hagop did, at around four o'clock in the morning when he'd run out to nab a few winks on the camp bed they had set up temporarily at the back of the garage the first night; it had been there ever since.

Hagop would sleep for four hours, then leave for the Museum for his day job, scarfing on the way the contents of a brown paper bag that Baran would leave for him in the passenger seat of his car every morning. Tacos, stuffed and rolled vegan omelets, vegetable tempura, maki, donuts, ice cream cones, always a big cup of coffee—it was the best meal of the day. Hagop savored his drive to La Brea. Full, he slammed the door of his car and, burping, entered his second time capsule at eight o'clock on the dot.

Hagop Bates knew the Ice Age like the back of his hand. He'd spent ten years now dedicating most of his days to it, eight to six, minus his lunch break, which he now spent sleeping, weekends, and two weeks of vacation per year. He had extracted sharp weapons fused to steel jawbones, he had taken out bone lace, vegetal membranes, traces of life, he had analyzed rock, metal, precious stones reduced to dust, but he had never seen anything resembling what was spread out that morning under his microscope.

In the middle of the night, he had lifted out the object, which had finally been freed. With Baran's help, swearing and huffing profusely, he had succeeded in hoisting up the block, which had to weigh at least eighty kilograms. They looked at it, turning it over, assessing it. Maybe he was tired, distracted, or already preoccupied with the signs that he thought he had seen, but the fact was that he reached the internal mass more quickly than he expected, removing a shard about the size of .03 mm pencil lead. This was a mistake for a technician of his caliber, but a boon for the litho-preparer in him that had never been completely snuffed out. He had been preparing the sample all morning. He held back from making premature hypotheses, but the block looked a lot like some kind of aluminum alloy. The lab work would confirm or disconfirm his intuition. While waiting, he was eager to get back to working in Baran's garage and could no longer really tell which time capsule he was in. He'd stopped knowing the moment the object had been fully extracted.

Baran Blizzard's house had been the epicenter of his mental activity for weeks now. The camp bed stunk of sweat and soil, his clothes and hair reeked of hydrogen sulfur, his nails were always black underneath despite frequent handwashing, his vision had gotten used to the greenish light, which he needed to dim by covering it with a tarp every night. He could no longer go out during the day without sunglasses; he could no longer tolerate even sunset.

When they had the perfectly clean parallelepiped at their feet, disinterring ancient alluvia and countless subterranean concoctions, when they had it before their eyes—naked, blinding, excessively geometric—they understood they'd had a life that would not be coming back.

There was no questioning the lab results. The block was pure aluminum. A monolith. It came from space. That wasn't such a big deal. What was, however, was that it didn't come from our solar system. And it certainly didn't come from the past, even if you were to count back by billions of years.

But it was there, unmistakable.

That was a fact.

Baldo Casino

The carpet is thick. As Adrian moves forward he feels as if he's treading on a layer of snow that's blanketed the ground overnight. There are three centimeters of blown wool—gray, with notes of pearl and oyster shell—designed to withstand high foot traffic and regular cleaning, which have been professionally installed onto the floor, three high-quality centimeters that separate the floorboard from the sole of his shoe.

Adrian doesn't get tired of returning to the hotel lobby after his morning walk and noting that wellbeing is a question of shock absorption. You can pick up on luxury immediately through your feet. Gold, chandeliers, fireplaces, the general forms of elegant décor, and door frames come next, once you've made first contact with your plantar sensors.

In Baldo Casino's lobby every morning, matter gives way under his footsteps. It subsists and fades, accompanying him silently until the bottom of the stairs. Preceding and responding to him, attentive to the smallest of his movements, it's a presence, an echo, almost a mind. The thoughtfulness of the Baldo Casino lobby's carpet is cause for discreet wonderment and Adrian is pleased to start each day with it. The path to the lakefront, the deep water, the clear air, the massive mountain on the opposite shore, somber and crowned with white, only take on their actual dimensions when he penetrates the hotel lobby, open to everybody and separated from the outside by a revolving door whose function is not so much to separate the two spaces but to make them pivot into each other with the flow. A suitcase, bellboy, client, driver, and seagull are so many chances to blend together air with different properties, to add the comfortable lining of human artifice to the rock's icy mantle. The lavishness of palaces comes down to this modest exchange, lost only on mujiks and new mafiosi.

Adrian isn't a misanthrope. He picks up his mail daily, devoting an hour of his morning to do so, he receives people in the large drawing room, always offering the deepest armchairs to his interlocutors when they announce and introduce themselves punctually. He keeps up the conversation, no matter what direction it takes. Investing, botany, industry, the new automobile, the infrathin, or railway history, it doesn't matter, he's an expert on everything. To keep the conversation in the gaseous, not completely soporific state that's demanded by relationships of a certain cultivation, all that's required is a quotation, a statistic, an anecdote, or putting on a smile. He observes more than he listens. The positioning of a foot, the angle of a head, the relation between someone's mouth and hair, provides him with more information than could be extracted from an overly constructed sentence or a perfectly clear clause.

Real conversations, those can only be had while walking. With butterflies, when your body is sufficiently focused on its own movements, your consciousness sufficiently absorbed by the hunt, words inadvertently hit upon essential topics and are able to pirouette freely, taking shape unhindered. In that moment, you need to be accompanied by a familiar free spirit who's quick to flight and in sync with you, like a household deity or like a Vera, a Luce, a Lena, a Lucette, a Lucinda, a Dolores who, all grown up and passionate, will resume childhood where it had stopped. Better than any story.

If Adrian has moved into the Baldo Casino for good, taking up six lake-facing rooms on the fifth floor, a kitchen, two drawing rooms, with a desk in his bedroom, it's because he knows that past a certain age (say, twelve years old), you only live in transitory spaces. He sold his palazzo in the Val d'Ema with its square terraced garden and bushes cut into cocks and cones, he let go of a dacha, of an entire estate on the banks of the Volga, crackling with ice and drowning in the honey of a spring sun, he entrusted to speculators an enclosed vineyard in the heart of the Côte de Nuits, he placed his Manhattan penthouse with a view of the park in the hands of a real estate agent, he put up for auction many pieces of furniture and objects, and two old cars whose hoods were ornamented with statuettes of a gold-plated woman-dragonfly about to take off. Because the world is emptying out and there's only one way to accompany and counteract its movement, because gold is a convention and a chemical element that, as with blood, is inappropriate to let congeal.

Wearing Bermuda shorts when you're more than sixty years old isn't inappropriately childish. To describe this military item of clothing invented overseas by the Navy in this way, you'd need to believe in time, or to only consider a hunt to be challenging if the tools are heavy and lethal. Mushrooms and lepidopterans require a light material, but the sum of the territories that they invite you to explore is much vaster than anything a poacher sprays with bullets in some random corner of a forest. Mycology and lepidopterophilia are thus two good reasons to choose short pants that allow for ease of movement and free airflow. With over-the-knee socks, you're perfectly adapted to dry or humid prairies and to mountains. Moreover, childhood being less a time period and more of a space and a fantasy, it is never anachronistic to wear its clothes. By putting himself through this ritual, he allows himself to open secret doors and access certain curio cabinets, shapely and colorful.

There are no creatures—including Ovid's—more capable of metamorphoses than butterflies. The most common one molts two or three times after becoming a larva and before the imago stage. They change skin, shape, color, and mode of locomotion several times per life—so many shifts in narrative, so many opportunities for perception and enrichment. From articulated crawling to unpredictable flight, they know how to do it all—even walking. Little Apollo, for instance, is happy most of the time to survey on foot the banks of streams lined with large gray stones bleached by the foam. Like an aristocrat from the court of Arden whom good manners forbid from flying, she climbs back up the raging flow on the tips of her six little prickly tarsi and only gives into temptation, if no male is in sight, in order to reach the tallest field scabious stalks.

On the rock, firmly, but unostentatiously, she sets down her four red, black-lined eye spots, her dark skeleton, and the grays of her open wings. As if it were the work of a lifetime. As a caterpillar she was a velvety black, covered in short hairs and marked on both sides by a stippled red line and blue patches. Her chrysalis was black interspersed with blue—silky, then powdery and white, bluish while drying. A simple empty shell after ten to thirty days of industrious activity.

Her capacity to disarrange her organs, contained inside silky armor, has always been the stuff of Adrian's dreams. Since before he was six, and after turning forty, and then some, he's continued to ponder this talent, jealously hidden from the world, for extending antennae, shrinking down mandibles and the digestive tube, enlarging the eyes and brain, and preparing the little soft frippery that the imago, once finally liberated, will, clinging to the underside of a leaf or the stalk of its plant, let hang pitifully for a half-hour, that it will inflate with air and blood until it becomes wings, identifiable and recognizable as the four works of art and engineering that they are.

Witnessing the emergence of a butterfly remains one of the most expansive experiences that he has ever lived through. Adrian keeps entirely clear in his mind the memory of an improvised larvarium set up in one of the disused bathrooms of an estate too large to be maintained. A memory so precise that it stings: he can't call it up the way you would a mountain trout at the end of a fishing line—leaping, iridescent, wild—without feeling the heat rise in his cheeks and hands once again. The same heat. This is why he doesn't believe either in time or in loss, and why, every morning from spring till the beginning of winter, he scours the slopes and ridges of the neighboring mountains, the edges of his lake. To save, by trapping them in his net, the cabbage butterflies there had once been so many of, which he no longer crosses paths with except sporadically, through his formidable intuition and knowledge. It's for this, and for the transfer of a living butterfly from a cotton net to the complex net of human memory—for this and for the feeling of having the Baldo Casino's carpet sink under his feet—that he still wakes up with the sun each day, as if there had to be, somewhere, someone still capable of reading his notes and making use of them.

Unless it was for his own pleasure, that of reliving, without the inevitable dross, those scenes so dear to his heart. He reshuffles the cards. Like a larva in the midst of transforming, deceptively still, serene, free to create all kinds of monstrosities from safe inside its flexible and resistant shell, he examines a detail and bestows disproportionately precise proportions upon it, he gathers a slice of life, a long stretch of boredom, into six short legs, he draws out a caress, a feeling or a leaf blooming, a bud forming, into as many organs, he condenses two or three events over the course of time into compact, suitably hairy sacs, he recollects his dreams and breathes into them, tracing their venation, casting lead, going through colors, coming up with his stumpy wings. He makes the game up. Everything is enclosed and packed into the gangue made of threads that look like rock. He spends his afternoons bent over his index cards, inside his lamp's magical circle, at the lightweight desk he brought over from England along with a bedframe and whist table. He takes his tea like the Russians, at six. And afterward, concerns himself only with preparing his insomnia.

His life is as orderly as that of a retired civil servant. His only excess lies in his encyclopedic nature. Thus, for Adrian to, after meticulously crossing the hotel lobby, look through the daily issue of *The Courier* without registering anything, to make the usual gesture of grabbing two or three papers from the newspaper table whose headlines he tries to force himself to read before heading up the stairs to the fifth floor, to stumble across a booming front page and not understand it, to come back and duly note, without believing it, the permanent extinction of *Iolana iolas*, is to founder in a well. The Iolas blue can't have disappeared.

The world is in relation with its story like memory is with the body—a series of bridges, of thrown stems, lance-like, of intertwined and enlaced tendrils where it's impossible to tell where they start or end or what void they inhabit and traverse. A hole in his heart's reality—the only reality—this was what the news could provoke if he didn't immediately question it. *Iolana iolas* is the cornerstone of one of his most beautiful, replayed pieces of augmented life. The arbor in the park, too big to be surveilled, the arbor, dark at midday, covered by a dense vine, a square garden with soft soil, and his Luce, his Lucette, his Lola, Loliu, Lolina buried in the leaves, leaning over the snail that, slimy, is gliding between his pectorals, loose hair brushing up against erect nipples. Adrian lying on the cool earth, Adrian burning up. The light puddling up on Lola's young breasts, so fair, on her loins, the sweetness of her crisp thatch and of what followed, and, later, much later, because they were already taking their time, in the stillness and the warmth, the *Iolana iolas* that came to drink, two legs on the edge of the navel's lip, the precious substances that had been secreted. Blue scales and powder on the blond down, the belly.

Iolana iolas can't have vanished. Filled up on juices, it's taken off in whimsical flight, its trajectory and goal known only to it; it's covered an enormous amount of ground, it's made numerous detours and has retreated under a fern, to the back of a nettle, but it hasn't disappeared.

Because if it has, then so has the woody honeyeyed skin of his beloved, her delicate fuzz, the taste of her mouth, their playing hooky, their life under the leaves and in the arms of the vine. And gone with them the rectilinear path in the national forest of Galm from forty years later, the only stroke of clear light among this panoply of blacks, dark greens, and new growth. The only straight line amid the uncertain interlacing of animal traces, the only sun-kissed clearing—warm, vibrant, buzzing with insects whose steps and adventures had been accompanied by the Iolas blue, the ambler, as if they were all Adrian and Lola, permanent and changed, their fingers intertwined under the same, unforgettable, perhaps even vaster, arbor.

It numbered in the dozens. The world was expanding. Through what hole could it have suddenly fled?

Adrian flew up the stairs, no longer glancing at the newspapers tucked under his arm. He opened his drawers and dove in. He began rummaging through his filing cards as if they were fresh loam, known for a long time and frequently turned over, whose smells guide you and make you lose your head. He randomly found whole, intact index cards, detailed and perfectly written—the hawk moth, the lesser purple emperor, the purple emperor, the violet fritillary, the great banded grayling, the small heath, the brassy ringlet—which were all in their place, according to their common names, admirably legible. The card for the Spanish fritillary, *Euphydras desfontainii*, had a stain, a brown-edged white ring. The one for the hermit, *Chazara briseis*, was burnt, flames had consumed a quarter of it. But it wasn't just the *Nymphalidae* family, and not every individual was affected, it was also the southern marbled skipper and the Warren's skipper, the ink of their descriptions was partially erased, you could only make out the downstrokes, the bodies of the vowels had pulled away, impossible to make out. The large heath, the scarce fritillary, the southern comma (three more *Nymphalidae*) only had their names and annotations left—"Müller, 1764, Linnaeus, 1758, Cramer, 1775." Adrian found nothing but yellowed blank cards for the pigmy skipper and the scarce heath. He took a deep breath and narrowed his search to the *Lycaenidae*, finding many of the lycaenids to be perfectly conserved: a variety of whites, the holly blue, the Provençal short-tailed blue, the short-tailed blue, the Osiris blue, the scarce large blue, and then, where *Iolana iolas* should have been, a space the thickness of a missing card. A quarter-millimeter of emptiness.

He was hit by a momentary fit of motionless vertigo. As staggering as an aphasic episode. He touched his throat and passed his hand over his bald skull. He grabbed his desk's cornice, made an effort to get up, then collapsed down onto his bed, near the telephone. He relied on his conjuring ritual and recited the conjugation, in Russian, of the irregular verb "to be" backwards and forwards before asking the concierge if he would be so good as to send for an ambulance.

In the vehicle, lurching gently, separated from the smooth and gleaming asphalt—the same gray as the lake—by four all-season tires and the full height of the stretcher and the flexibility of the fabric, Adrian said to himself that luxury was indeed a question of shock absorption, but that, under certain circumstances, and not necessarily the best ones, the feet were not the first judges.

Thus, stretched out, he exited through the revolving door—triggering for the second time that day a gaseous exchange between two worlds not quite sealed off from each other, barely twenty minutes after having tread on the carpet of the Baldo Casino in the opposite direction for fifteen years—feet first, a hole in his files.

The oxygen undoubtedly helped him find

something tender in this situation that Vera, his Luce, his Lucette, his Lucinda, his Dolores—having returned to take his childhood into her arms where she had left it, intact, her long hair still undone—would have found so sad that she would have smiled.

Adrian, you always make such a fuss over *such* small departures.

Big Dogs

"It's not a huge loss."

"There's no such thing as a small loss in these matters. Lose the equivalent of a fingernail clipping and you'll find your treatment room freshly wallpapered after a weekend at the beach."

"At the beach?"

"It's a figure of speech, Syriakov. Find the clipping before it sucks you in like goulash. I've seen people bigger than you disappear and turn into a puddle. Where did you put the oats?"

"In the locked cabinet, take the key."

"Since when does the cooling system not work?"

"It's been two weeks. What are you going to do, Aliona Ilinitchna?"

"Feed the horses and inspect the stalls. As for you, continue your search, use your head and be clever enough to keep me from having to alert the Brigade."

Aliona Ilinitchna Belova unlocked the cabinet, grabbed the blue plastic bucket by the twine that served as a handle, and plunged an expert hand into the grain stocks. She filled it up two thirds of the way, taking care to make sure nothing spilled out, and passed through the treatment room door heading toward the stalls.

The courtyard, soaked by the overnight rain, looked pathetic. Remains of boiled potatoes floated like eyes in a mud purée. The foot traffic of men and animals had dug out deep ruts where the water stagnated, oily and swathed in shades of bronze. With each step, Aliona Ilinitchna's brown boots sank into the doughy mixture with a voluptuous sucking sound. Her breath projected white clouds ahead of her, which she traversed as she moved forward. The air quality was much better than it had been a decade earlier. Aliona was inwardly glad for this assessment, reached nearly every morning. She could distinctly remember the color and thick taste of the mornings from before, of the bland afternoons spent in lockdown.

Leveling needed to happen on dry days, placing planks down on the most frequented walkways, from the treatment room to the stables, from the stables to the fields, the quarry, the pool. The slabs in the rest of the courtyard needed to be sealed together and the drainage ditches enlarged. Lining them with ground-up slate could improve the outflow. She didn't have the manpower or the means to carry out the work that had piled up over the years. The center no longer stirred as much interest as it had at its opening. The hour of glory was past, and with it, the interest of sponsors. Time had taken a toll on her as well, and if her condition was far from being like that of the deformed courtyard she was crossing, a bucket on the end of her arm, she had lost her freshness and the persuasive force that brings in investors. Her radiance had dimmed, her work was slower, her passion deeper but less infectious. She had gotten tired of the public.

She came to the front of the barn whose door had ended up becoming completely warped and noted that the little window was still not covered up. She glanced over at the hay barn's struts and breathed in deeply, her nose turned toward the dormer overflowing with that year's hay. This first whiff whetted her appetite and called attention to all the stable's living smells. Warm, dense, as welcoming as the animals woken up by the smell of the oats and their owner who brought them.

Unlike the center's other modules—except for the laboratory and the treatment room, which were rigorously maintained according to regulation—the stable was Aliona's personal source of pride. She adored her horses. Her fifty small, muscular bodies, her living herd, wilder than partridges, more domesticated than the goats that, during the summer, would graze in the planters full of chives that she had put away in her room, the window wide open.

They welcomed her with upright ears, shaking their manes and calling out. She had a special gesture, a sweet remark or word, or a carrot peel for each of them. During her first round through the building, she would speak to them as she poured out oats into the mangers. She would wait for them to plunge their heads into the troughs, to blow on the last flecks, then she would retrace her steps and unlock all the latches, leaving it to them to push open the door with the bridges of their noses, and, stamping at the ground, hungry for fresh air, join her at the end of the stable.

She knew each one of them individually, down to the most hidden combinations of their DNA. She had made them.

Her first two victories, black pinto toveros from excellent genetic stock, were always first in line to nibble her fingers. They pushed their white blazes against her knees, rearing up and hurling their legs at her waist so that she would finally open the panel that led to the field. Aliona put up with their demonstrations without ever stopping her observations of the others. All she needed to do was to walk the length of the central walkway to know everything about their health and their states of mind. No limping, no respiratory or urinary problems, no irritation could make it past her watchful eye and her intuition. When assembled together, they horsed around in front of the closed door, but once she let them loose, each horse walked calmly in front of her, throwing glances at her with blue eyes, brown eyes, shaking their heads or letting out a sigh for her benefit. The mares weren't to be outdone when it came to seduction. The last little mare, a filly barely two years old who gracefully wore her chocolate-colored and freshly washed hair, had taken on the habit of hitting her left boot with her hoof three times—systematically, unhurriedly—before crossing the doorway. She would then lift her neck to see what effect she'd had and, every time, Aliona expected her to fire off a wink or to show her teeth. But the filly would turn her nostrils away and set off into the open air with a little trot, delighted to have piqued her owner's curiosity.

She didn't rub all of them down every day, but after a day of work, she had them go to the pool to relax their muscles and soothe their fatigue. A ramp of blow dryers awaited them at the pool's exit and finished warming them before the evening ration and a night spent in fresh litter. Her horses were athletes and she treated them as such. Athletic wonders that had come out of her test tubes and her forward-looking imagination.

During the period when the soil was so worn out that it was no longer possible to sustain even a quarter of the livestock that was thought to be needed, during the period when coal and refined fuel vehicles had disappeared for lack of resources and oil, her miniature horses had appeared to be an elegant solution to the problem of local transportation.

Hitched up, they could tow light freight cars, carriages, wagons, and canvas-covered stage-coaches for transporting humans. A clover patch was all that was needed to feed a herd of sixty crea-tures through the winter. During the dry season, their modified metabolic system allowed them to live off a half-gallon of water per month *per capita*. They digested dried-up végétaline, silverines, and wood ash, which provided them with the neces-sary calcium.

They did not fart.

The number of orders had skyrocketed after the endurance test results and the complete table of power-energy-endurance ratios were published in *Nature and Adaptation*. Aliona Ilinitchna Belova had had to reassess her set-up, to recruit, train, and produce on a scale she wouldn't have ever dared dream of. The investors clamored at her door, assistants presented themselves, unsolicited, by the hundreds, trainers tried to outdo each other in dexterity, men, in their romantic declarations. (Women were more discreet.)

All of Siberia wanted in, Australia offered fantastic advances in exchange for the guarantee of being supplied first. The ranchers of the American West had snatched up the first shipment at auction, Europe, after taking some time to think things over, threw itself into the race by appointing eminent trainers who were determined to lend a hand and identify the best stock. Alina Ilinitchna didn't need their expertise. She had developed the most economical cloning technique in the world by herself in her dusty Bratsk laboratory, without anyone's help or blessing, and she intended to keep a tight rein on it. She didn't regret her choices. Looking at the rickety hay barn, the badly lit grange, and the muddy mash of potatoes at her feet, she felt at peace with the past, and she would stay this way for as long as her fifty steeds frolicked in the field before her eyes.

If, on that most bleak and blessed day when she found yellow lichen in the smoky wood, you had told her that it would be the vector of hope and of the Renaissance, she wouldn't have even cracked a smile. She'd already seen more than her fair share of crazy shamans and their predictions.

They had descended from Yakutia by the dozens during the exorcism wave, headed to Moscow with their handcarts and straggly beards. Undaunted, destined. The opposite of orators. They nonetheless subjected entire villages to their prophetic visions which were bombastic, but, above all, tinged with common sense.

Walls and seas of fire invaded their minds. In the dark tents where they carried out the ceremonies, you could hear the sinister cracks of tree trunks that were pulverized the moment they were touched, you could feel the burning waves unfurl, one after the other, invading the space, ravaging it, you could hear the animals running away, the beating of paws and hooves and wings, cries, whistles, death rattles—the tent was shaken by everything that was trying to escape and those who could fly didn't always succeed in doing so. The hole at the top was narrow, under attack, obstructed. The shaman himself, on the edge of asphyxiation, had increasing difficulty digging a tunnel in the black smoke, an inverted chimney through which he exited before taking off for the regions higher up that were less affected and bringing back, in his magic bellows, something to chase away the pestilence and ardent death from the tent. The villagers emerged singed, their eyes red and frightened by what they had encountered. The self-evident truth.

She had escaped from lockdown one afternoon. She was too bored. She slipped outside by crawling on all fours past the watchman's post and took off for the woods. It was only a few months—maybe eight—after the shamans had come through. Everything had indeed burned down. Millions of acres of forest, billions of animals, only a few hundred humans in this region mostly uninhabited by the great apes. She avoided their fate by climbing, just in time, into an ancient An-2 biplane loaded up past capacity, which nonetheless managed to take off in less than three hundred meters, a fire lit under its ass. Through the window she was smushed up against, barely breathing, unable to make out the earth below, which was swallowed up in a smoke more solid than sea ice, she saw the paint on the wings blister. Once the tank was empty, five hundred kilometers south of Bratsk, they landed on the banks of the Baikal, its waters red.

And then she came back, on horseback and on foot next to the horse, provisioned with two heavy bags and a light weapon. Thirty-five kilometers from Bratsk, she reached a forest ranger outpost that she knew of, rummaging through a layer of ash a meter thick to recover whatever remained of it. A misshapen moka pot, cutlery melted into a ball, the skeleton of a radio, the handles from five drawers. She pitched her completely gray felt tent to the west of what was left of this wooden structure, in a circular clearing she spent a week making, removing the remains of the burns. It was at her door, at the beginning of the third week, that the team of men picked her up and brought her to Bratsk's Camp B, where all the Revenants were to be rounded up by order of the authorities. Aliona Ilinitchna Belova was surprised that there were still, or rather, already, militiamen ready to execute orders. She showed her papers, her diplomas, the contents of her briefcases, which she always kept at her side, and obtained luxury lodging (fifteen square meters with a kitchen in a brick tower) and a pass for the hydroelectric power plant's decontamination center.

The dilapidated complex had never been good for much. The mercury had saturated the catchment waters a decade before the great fires. Since then, they'd been enriched with selenium, ammonia, nitrates, and total nitrogen at absolutely forbidden levels. But the facilities were still usable and she was one of the only scientists in the region to have come back. She carried out the experiments she wanted to. Her only obligation was to join the other Revenants at the lockdown unit every afternoon. There were about thirty of them who hadn't known where to go when they left Irkutsk nor what to keep themselves busy with. Fatalistic forest rangers, peasants who preferred their burned-down farms to the burned-down farms of the people of Baikal, former plant employees, retirees who had been allocated a dacha they hoped to rebuild, fishermen suffering from mercury poisoning—trembling, half blind, half insane, used to their fish, whose scales turned fuchsia when they were taken out of the water.

The measure had been imposed by Moscow under the pretext of protecting the population from emissions whose toxicity had been evaluated as being systematically too elevated after 2:00 PM. The official peak was set for 4:00 PM and you could go about your business again after 6:00 PM. This was, of course, absurd. Their goal was to maintain the illusion of control while maintaining real control of bodies—the very essence of power.

The day of the escape, she'd had enough. Of the mustachioed imbecile who guarded Camp B, his feet on the counter, fiddling with his whiskers and with his cartridge pouch in turn, of her desperate research on fireweed's capacity for rapid regeneration, of the wilted blueberries she dissected day after day before cooking them, of the *Lupus alba* and *Equus caballus* cells that took too long to reproduce.

She wanted to go on a walk in the woods. Among the tree trunks—black and upright, intact, lined up, fragile like relics, like burned up matches. She wanted to stir up the dust while walking, to feel her weight sink into the ash, to feel her breath filter particles, to hear the sound of her voice.

A few green tufts had popped up again here and there showing their heads. Thorny or downy, the moss was reappearing in patches like scabies, too slowly to constitute a real hope, too persistent not to be one after all. The different shades of green flickered in a palette of monotonous grays. The eye instinctively revived itself from these patches of color. Each encounter was a way of drinking, of picking up on water and life in the midst of desolation, of telling the moon apart from the earth.

She had not seen the yellow spot of lichen at first, but smelled it. A cool drop in a tepid pool. She followed the thread of sensation, roaming, led by her nose through the still air, doing her best to tell where this splash of light was in the gloomy carpet of undergrowth. She went in circles around the point of initial impact, the specific spot where the smell had hit her—like a hunting dog, she set off making spirals that tightened of their own accord, until she came face to face with the yellow, dazzling, branching, veined, visibly living body.

She immediately identified it—a myxomycetes plasmodium—she wasn't sure which kind exactly, but it had woken up and fed itself, that much was certain. It pulsated. Yesterday's rain shower must have drawn it out of dormancy, it was young and very active if she was to judge from the traces left on the branch to which it stuck. It had enveloped, liquified, and digested a mushroom twenty centimeters across. Its pseudopods extended in all directions, looking for new prey.

She had removed it from its mount spontaneously, without thinking. Maybe because its freshness had shocked and seduced her and she wanted to take it—this new body that showed off its indiscreet color with abandon—with her, as proof, a guarantee, a promise.

Back in the laboratory at the decontamination center, she had confined and fed it in a petri dish barely big enough for it. Then she had forgotten about it.

Two days was all it took for the plasmodium to escape from its box and crawl to her blueberry reserves, swallowing her fireweed and tasting all the cultures she had started. She found it rolled into a ball on the lab ceiling, letting long, translucid filaments dangle to the floor, visibly famished. When, from atop a stepladder missing two steps, she had peeled it off, she had been surprised by its weight and the resistance it offered up. During the time it took to come down the six steps, paying attention to the ones that were missing, the plasmodium had affixed itself to her hands in a disagreeable way, she had to nearly throw it onto the lab bench to free herself of it. She put it into a bucket, poured some oats onto it, and began observing the substance that remained on her fingers under a microscope. And what she saw unsettled her.

The myxomycete plasmodium had assimilated a quantity of animal cells without digesting them. Aliona's first reaction was to wash her hands energetically. The second was to open a detailed investigation into its movements over those last two days. She discovered that it had sucked up the bacterial soups before stumbling onto the stem cells of the Siberian wolf and the Yakut horse that she'd cultured in her rudimentary heat chamber. She returned to her microscope and the absurd idea that would change her life crossed her mind.

It took her months to bring together the conditions of its realization. Months of attempts, failures, invalidated hypotheses—months of obstinacy.

She pulled out all the stops, filling out heaps of forms, making both official and unofficial requests to obtain the mature ova she needed. She even went herself to look for three solid mares at a stud farm in Sedanovo. Over burning hot tea, chewing on a slice of greasy, flavorful meat, Aliona Ilinitchna had spoken for hours to a breeder couple. Three months later, the embryos born of an *Equus* ovum and of the assemblage produced by the plasmodium were implanted into the surrogate mother. Aliona Ilinitchna woke up with a start, eleven months later, in the middle of a warm night, distressed by a premonitory dream. She ran to the stable improvised in the room adjoining the laboratory and she knew before entering that it had all been decided. The air was heavy with the usual smell of foaling—milk, blood, liquid dung mixed in with the litter—and the placentas had been delivered all clumped together as if the mares had gathered to share their progeniture and their pain. The burst sacs and the silky placentas lay at the center of the circle they formed, and, at the heart of this revolution, six little bodies were stretched out. Two were alive.

Orpa and Ozga, with their white blazes and white socks, their intelligent heterochrome eyes, were still her favorites.

They grazed at top speed, leaving perfectly clean recursive fractal figures behind them, they played without injuring themselves, bathed in the dry dust like house sparrows, and never charged without reason.

Maybe because she gave them all her attention during the months following their birth, feeding them herself with a baby bottle in her hand, grooming and bathing them after each long journey, Orpa and Ozga never tried to run away. The forty-eight others all escaped whenever they were able to. In a group, by themselves, in twos or in threes, they leapt over the fence before she had it electrified, kicked down the too fragile stalls, went through tiny holes, plotted, hid themselves before breaking through the smallest breach into a great gallop. Syriakov had to use all of his wits when he took the herd grazing in the woods. He carried three lassos and a fishnet with him, coming back complaining that he didn't have a dog at his disposal. Over and over again, they had to leave in the middle of the night to look for a lost one that they'd sometimes find at their heels, drawn by the sound and by the light of the flashlights, its teeth bared.

This was not the reason, however, that the little horses' popularity had come to an end.

Immersed in her memories, Aliona Ilinitchna looked at the land around her. The shiny and solid bodies of the pine trees that had passed through flame gleamed under the morning sun. They were destroyed, yet still standing, a tuft of red needles here and there giving some sense of the lightness of the system that had enveloped and nourished them when they were still able to exchange water, gases, and nutrients with their environment. Reduced to their simplest structure, completely carbonized, they were still participating in the world, giving their fossilized image back to it, standing stubbornly, rebellious.

Aliona Ilinitchna was taking in this far off landscape when she saw Grizby, a beautiful three-year-old cream-colored centaur-like stallion, freeze before a small hillock in the middle of the field. His left leg raised, bent at a right angle, his ears tilted forward, trembling in their motionlessness. She smiled despite herself and whistled between her fingers. The horse had heard her, but didn't move, frozen in his alert position. Then, suddenly, he drove forward from his hindquarters, burying his nostrils into the soil and scratching at the ground like one possessed. She heard him blow into the hole he was enlarging, shaking with excitement, his tail high, chills running up and down his spine. Very quickly, he raised his head, triumphant, a multicolored lemming between his gritted teeth. He broke its neck by throwing it up in the air and catching it again adroitly, violently. He broke into a calculated trot, went around the field once, then came to deposit his prey at his owner's feet. An homage. Aliona stroked and thanked him, placed the body into her hunting bag. Syriakov wouldn't have approved, but Syriakov had a fixed idea of the instinct reserved for each species.

He had gotten used to the size of the little horses, because that was the least strange thing in the world left by the great fires, because one gets used to what's aberrant if it looks like what one has always known, because one is accustomed to own-ers' caprices when one has been a groom for fifty years. He loved them in his own way, with a kind of wild distance that didn't exclude intimacy. Aliona had seen him sleep in the hay to keep an eye on a mare worked up at the imminence of her foaling. She had seen him prechew carrots and give, bit by bit, to weak foals, the mush in the hollow of his hand. She had seen him hit, in the belly, an animal that had swelled up to get out of wearing its harness. He had slaughtered the ones who were beyond help. Syriakov was the only one to stay behind after the golden age of little horses. Not for her pleasure, but that of the horses, who had seduced him, no matter what he said. Without batting an eye, he filed their teeth and the hard calluses that formed on their front hooves. He accepted whatever had to do with their bodies. But if a zealous little horse brought him a still-warm mole or baby rabbit, it would get whipped on the spot.

Aliona Ilinitchna felt an indefinable discomfort for no particular reason. Perhaps she shouldn't have put Syriakov in contact with the plasmodium. She knew he was unable to stand this thing that was neither a lichen, nor an animal, nor a plant, nor even an organism—strictly speaking. He had always been reluctant to feed it and be alone with it. He had only shown disgust at its capacities. To move without the help of limbs, to think without a brain, to live without a heart, to not die—these were, for him, intolerable absurdities.

She had a bad feeling hearing the door of the treatment room close behind her. She knew that the little horses, despite their phenotypical perfection, were unprecedented animals, somewhat unpredictable. She had expected, from the beginning, for there to be variation in certain traits, a reinforcement of their sociality, a recomposition of the group hierarchy, an alteration of the stress response. Beneath the appearance of a miniature horse, they took after the Siberian wolf. Their flight instinct was overtaken and contradicted by a predatory drive. What she didn't know yet was how the plasmodium itself was beginning to transmit its genetic capacities.

Syriakov tottered across the courtyard. He was struggling against a weight that seemed to be pulling his arm down to the ground. Aliona, in the middle of the field, surrounded by her fifty perfect little loves, watched him advance, breathless.

He was the only one moving in a world that had coagulated. Him, and the shapeless mass that encircled his hand and arm up to the shoulder and projected cirri and vigorous flagella around itself. They slapped the air with the cracking and hissing of a riding crop. Syriakov advanced, blinded by the blows and the raging tentacles grabbing onto his hair. He kicked. He threw his arm far away from him only to have it come back smack dab in the middle of his face. He reeled. The plasmodium swarmed and grunted using his voice. Aliona, motionless, stunned, waited without thinking. Out of touch with everything except the implacable progression she was witnessing. Absorbed, sated. Beyond herself.

The only thing she noticed was that she was drawing her lips back over her teeth at the same moment, along with all the little horses around her, and that she was taking into her lungs the terrifying smell of the plasmodium's mature sexual spores.

Great Apes

They didn't speak. They vocalized to stay in contact in the thick fog. They were several meters apart from each other and the sounds they produced connected them to each other and to their territory, floating in the water vapor.

Each groome was a sonorous thread thrown toward the other, each response provided the relative position of the other members of the group, as well as specific information about the mood and activity of the moment. As a whole, the score outlined a detailed map of the present community and its smallest movements. Only the warning cry was likely to tear through this fabric and reveal, instantly, the nature and position of the disruptive event.

They didn't work, they had never worked.

They played, fed themselves, socialized and, with more or less curiosity, took part in the world, groomed themselves, blustered, learned from the elders, built things, equipped themselves with tools, remained outside all constraints. Their regime was one of nonchalance and strict economy.

They slept in nests. Remade each evening, broken down each morning.

They wore, as coats, the cold fog of the forest, the hot steam of the springs, filtered light, full light, the moon. They changed outfits up to six times a day. For jewelry, they turned to artifacts and the skill some of them had when it came to colors and crushed clay.

The world around them presented itself, new and continued, indefinite—when they found their pittance, it was complete, when they didn't, it was expandable. They moved around in it but did not explore it. No sense of limits came to drive or disturb their investigations. They plunged into a space without making a fuss or a record, without sounding it out save through the reach of their voices and the keenness of their senses. As long as they were inside the sonorous fabric, they didn't want for air, or earth, or sky, or anything that grew and drew between the two. When the signal punctured the fabric and let the accident surge through, acoustic agitations swirled around the breach, thrown on top of the snag following a predetermined protocol whose intensity was calibrated to the urgency of the first cry and to the echo provided by the intrusive obstacle or action. If a buffalo passed by, its trace was announced, then covered up by a tiled structure whose angle of construction depended on the position and knowledge of the sounder of the alert. A good lookout needed to be accompanied by a good crier. And a good warning cry needed to go completely through the event, in one way or another, so that the responses might latch on firmly, crossing, intertwining, and end by mending the material. An encounter with a buffalo and the response to it were over in a dozen seconds.

An incursion was the only phenomenon liable to disrupt their murmurs and their singing. Neither sickness, nor death, nor birth, which they would welcome in silence or lulled by the sounds of everyday activities, gave rise to the slightest excess. Some of them were noisy out of a taste for grand gestures.

A certain idea of lyricism, excess, humor, or of social provocation would suddenly stir them up. They would then be able to sweep the group up into an unmoving kind of farandole,[1] an eddy where they weren't so much its center as its exposed source. The moment would arrive and disappear like a mood, without affecting in the slightest the speed or nature of the flux that was enveloping them. It would break out, a color that would reveal itself spontaneously, soaking the assembly, inclining it, enriching it with a tone that disappeared almost as soon as it had been set down.

They did not get bored.

The reporting of slow approaches, which weren't ignored, melted into the social fabric without mangling it. The presence of larger, more flavorful leaves, of a more tender bamboo, of a salty spring, of a bouquet of anti-parasitic nettles, was gently incorporated. Neither designated nor commented upon, but understood.

They climbed, slid, rolled around on the ground and changed branches with the same

---

1. A farandole is a type of Provençal dance.

flexibility and ease with which they tore down a shrub in one slow, sedate movement. They were vegetarian, precise, powerful, able to stop a charging hippopotamus with a single strike with their chest, as well as to extract a tick out of the thick hair of a furry chest and crush it between two lustrous leathery fingers.

Their eyes were velvety and gleaming. Only the lookouts would let the whites be seen.

They had let in the pale individual with the too-short arms who gravitated around them the way they would have recorded any other living body's persistence. The fact that it stayed for a long time at the edge of the world allowed them to identify its form and the quality of its reactions. It was small, female. Neither her trace nor her appearance had ever set off an alarm, because she had presented herself, disheveled and stinking, like the open leaf of a tree fern. Barely moving more in the wind, barely more soaked by the rain. They got used to finding her at the feet of their nest every morning, to watching her touch and smell their dejecta, to hearing her maneuver clumsily behind their backs. They had observed her jerky, disruptive movements, noted the absence of facial expression, felt discomfort at the acidic stench that followed her everywhere.

The young ones had gone to get a closer look at her on several occasions. Her teeth were tiny, she rarely bared them. A stringy lichen grew on her skull. Her skin, which they had touched, was dry, cold. They had proposed several games, then lost interest. There was celery that needed peeling, an insect fluttering around, flamboyant—inspiration struck. The canopy called to them, they climbed on the vines and ran down the trunks. They made balls of leaves that they rolled against their teeth. The juice oozed. The group got going. It was time to nap. To groom. There were fresh shoots that needed tasting.

The flux was full of variations.

The groomes had begun by bouncing off her body as off a part of the landscape, an inedible object, mobile, some kind of animal presence, then, little by little, by dint of repetition, it became integrated into the threads. At first a bypassed mass, more or less inert and uniquely capable of deviating the wave, then, later on, a thinking organism, and finally, one day, they picked up on an emitted sound that was relatively close to that of a contact vocalization. The adults perked up their ears, the lookout turned toward the little female and their eyes met. Each of them examined the other's eyes with the sensation of being bound to a suspended vine about to break. She then tilted her head in greeting and voluntarily broke contact by throwing out a second, correct vocalization. The entire group heard her. Adda responded, Imo confirmed, and the welcome sound passed through all ears and against everyone's fur before returning charged with the particular energy of the attention it carried. The very next instant, everyone was en route to construct the nests—night was coming.

Shaken, Duane stayed motionless in the twilight. At sunset, the high-altitude forest looked like a huge, deserted chateau. Creaking, piercing whimpers, and dull and sudden bangs came out of nowhere. The fog blended in with the Spanish moss that hung from the branches like giant spiderwebs. Shadows wove in and out between these sad sheets, whistling drafts chased after them, the cold fell on one's shoulders, touched the earth, and then, all at once, night was there, immense. A well.

Duane knew from experience that it was better not to wander through the cloudy forest between nightfall and dawn. All that she had left was a shovel and a bit of tent to cover the hole in which she would bury herself on site, just as the group would go off to sleep. She did not drag her feet in getting to work, preparing the basic cavity, covering it with branches, tying down the canvas and slipping in underneath before moonrise, if there was one. She then let the nocturnal theater play out above her head while sucking down the contents of a tube of food. The witches' cries didn't disturb her, nor did the snoring, or the barking. The only thing she still dreaded was being disturbed by something crawling. She always triple-checked the edging of her roof before letting herself slip into a porous sleep. Her dreams of vampires and the living dead were reinforced by the soundtrack outside, but its source was just her brain. Her brain, her knowledge, her imagination. The memory that she had of old performances and events poorly buried in the past returned almost every night with the animal cries, which she knew couldn't come from the throat of a werewolf, centaur, or three-headed guard dog. Nonetheless, the Styx flowed against her canvas, she heard its rustling. And each morning she noted its evaporation. The nocturnal river's disappearance invaded the landscape in the form of heavy stacks of steam that rose gradually—white, gray, translucent, then transparent, suddenly vanishing.

Locating the group was a relief. Duane was an accomplished tracker. She was confident she could locate their traces and take the paths they had blazed the previous evening. The group never moved more than three to four hundred meters from the last feeding station to their camp for the night. They couldn't get away from her or dissipate like a bunch of foam. Nonetheless, she only breathed freely once she had them in her sights and was watching their descent from the nests, their first delousings, their embraces.

She began to feel the envelope the moment she penetrated their circle, to feel it like a skin into which she was sliding in order to feel all the others and all the trees in it.

Her vocabulary had expanded, she mastered up to six grunted-roared vocalizations but, apparently, she didn't always use them appropriately. The surgical mask she wore constantly in their presence didn't help her make herself understood. The sounds came out muffled and reduced, the nuances got lost. To make up for it, she produced clicks and clacked consonants without phonation, which allowed her to introduce herself gently. Since she had reached the sanctuary, Duane was very careful about etiquette. She would have found it shocking to present herself unannounced without any oratory precautions. A sound of introduction, a gestural sign, a posture of approach was the bare minimum courtesy, when one wanted, as she did, to gain access to the teaching that they dispensed without thinking about it.

Duane had gone through one of the last wildlife corridors that connected the plain to the wooded mountain. A hedge of eucalyptus and crooked shrubbery lining a road that had been abandoned in favor of a four-laner which had eaten up the rest of the plateau's forest zone. She had entered into this shrubby tangle to collect wads of fur, to identify the broken twigs, carefully peeled trunks, cavities. And to flee from the deserts that the two strips of asphalt on either side of the hedge had become. She had moved forward one half-step at a time, attentive to all the smells, to the slightest rustling of which she wasn't the origin. At this point on her route, finding droppings, no matter how small, was a sign of life, a form of salvation, and the assurance that she shared at least one physiological structure with them. The many reassuring touches that the Eips doled out among themselves was no longer a mystery in her eyes. She had understood during her crossing of the corridor, and surely well before, how much the smallest sign of community, of similarity, of attention, could be calming as well as stimulating. In all likelihood, she had known this since birth, but without the keen awareness of it she was now compelled to have.

The first time the lookout had met her eyes, the first time that a juvenile had held out their arm to touch her with the back of their hand, the first time that Adda had allowed and ordered a grooming session, that she had touched her skin under the fur, the sensation had been the same—she had recognized it, emerging from the dawn of time, so intact and familiar to the point of being over-whelming. This fulgurant return of a self-evident truth was distinctively archaic, doubled with the presentiment of loss, with the keen intuition that she would never be sated with or weaned of this thing.

When it comes down to it, this was, perhaps, exactly what she had come looking for. More than the life sciences for which they have always been a source of evidence, more than the secret of their resilience—that a handful of humans had, after all, recognized and reinforced—more than their unpredictable faculty for slow adaptation, seem-ingly passive, more than their fatalism. Nothing but their touch.

With great effort, she had traversed the pla-teau, the sterile matrix, the increasingly smaller patches, the increasingly narrow corridors, cover-ing her face—the cap with the long visor pushed down on her head to avoid seeing too much of the sky, the side panels deployed as blinders—her breath constantly getting cut off, with only one thought on her mind. She had reached the sanctuary. As soon as she had, not seen, but smelled them, she understood that she would not carry out any research on them. That they would teach her everything, something at least, and that she wouldn't conduct even the most minor study. It had been another feint, a mental construct acquired in a world that was obsolete, an illusion, which had nonetheless led her all the way here, to the foot of the nests of the last species of hominids capable of surviving inside a postage stamp of natural space.

Duane had been born in an open environment. Very early on, she had seen birds fly, mammals run, and several fishes flee through holes in the riverbanks. The population density was so low in her preserve that the One Global Heath program had reached them belatedly and without much success. Throughout her entire childhood, she had known the arms of adults, body odors, interspecies physical games. There had been dogs in her community. Coyotes in the distance that one heard in the evening when the silence became even deeper and let sounds float across considerable distances. It was thanks to her Native origins that she was recruited later on by the Virtual Cynegetic Agency.

Her education was carried out through total immersion. She was plunged into reconstituted jungles for which the models no longer existed, to which infinite dimensions were assigned in exchange. The educational material was so effective that one could fall ill from a civet bite, an unnoticed thorn, or a puddle of stagnant water. She often injured herself, having to mend her clothes, cobble together containers and filters, learn to shelter herself and procure food. This period was so rich in life forms, colors, and traps of all kinds, that she was disoriented upon reaching the ground. The real one.

Her mission was to locate frugivore flying foxes that were suspected to have maintained their activity in patch AC40. She didn't understand at first that she had been dumped at the edge of the territory. The low stone wall in front of her was the material border, she knew, but it traversed a homogenous dead zone, arid on both sides. She had to camp there and wait for night to obtain some sign of wildlife and deduce from it which direction to take.

At the end of two months on the lookout, she discovered them assembled around a hundred wild mango trees and trees with nectar that were spread out across ten hectares. There were a handful of them. She observed them, following protocol. She placed nets, collected samples, weighed, tagged, and released nearly the entire colony. A young male died during handling. Duane felt the tiny heart racing against her fingers—she didn't have time to relax her grip, to present a drop of sugar—the flying fox expired, out of breath, releasing into the well of night the infinitesimal stream of air that had animated it an instant before and commanded an intelligent arrangement of membranes, bones, and ears to fly with its hands, drink with its head upside down, and wrap itself in its own arms.

She wrote up and submitted her report. Her conclusions were encouraging. The animal was a reliable vector due to its excellent performance in matters of dissemination and pollination. She provided dozens of pages comprising curves and diagrams, localization, displacements, the nocturnal and diurnal cycles of activity, the species' potential for territorial expansion. Her work was well-received, they congratulated her by interface just one week after reception, she felt recognized and flattered. That was another era.

Duane had never taken the Obstinates' activism seriously. The flying fox massacre opened her eyes. The killing drones that she felled with her slingshot and alarm pistol all bore the acronym OGH. By kicking the last one on the ground, destroying it, she signed the warrant for her arrest. She did so while smiling at the integrated mini camera before reducing what remained of the embedded motherboard and GPS to dust.

She buried the flying foxes. She stripped down, inspected herself, destroyed two electronic ticks ripped off her right earlobe and from between two toes, doused her clothes and left. The patches and the corridors became her natural environment. She never left anymore without cover, not even at night. The aseptic landscape of the matrix disgusted her, she couldn't tolerate the sight anymore. She was guided for lack of anything better by vast expanses devoid of smells and sounds, where the only movements taking place were those of the atmospheric weather balloons.

She had held herself back many times from puncturing these wineskins inflated with helium, which you couldn't even say circulated, as most of the time there wasn't enough of a draft to lift even a leaf. She advanced, lurking in the vegetal bowels, squeezed between these crushingly immobile masses. Hanging, as if it were a float, onto the hope of discovering, somewhere in a sliver of the mosaic, the trace, or better yet, the habitat of the Eips, of whom the Obstinates claimed to be the thought leaders.

Duane had never forbidden herself from reading anything. Her status as a tracker gave her access to any file that had something to do with real observations. Fascinated, she had read and reread *Notes and Reflections from the Ground* by Meryem Goodbear, the only openly Obstinate paleontologist. Eighty pages of directly transcribed facts, describing in detail the daily life of one of the oldest groups of free Eips, interspersed with personal reflections by the researcher, who tried to not conceal any dimension of her position as a disruptive agent, or her emotional or physiological conditions. She knew entire chapters by heart. Her recollection of the detailed lexicon of groomes at the end of the volume encouraged her to put out a decisive first vocalization. Since then, she hadn't ceased adapting and refining her knowledge, but had given up on recording it. The Eips had taught her not to leave behind any trace that wasn't inscribed in the flux, on the verge of disappearing. It wasn't dogma, simply the requirement for their form of life. And Duane no longer tolerated the idea that any of her creations might still be used for destruction. She had let herself be taken in once by the lure of conservation, she knew now that one only eats well while sitting, surrounded by food, hands, mouth, and ears open.

Adda had removed her mask during a delousing session. Without seeming to touch it, she unhooked the bit of earthy fabric, long ineffective, and let it fall to the ground like a peel. Duane immediately hid her nose and mouth in her elbow, but Adda continued the session without taking notice, passing and repassing her nails and hard fingers through the hair of the little female with the tense neck. When she felt her breathing freely, Adda turned her back to her, suddenly occupied with a bush of red berries, without even looking at her bare face. The young Gwongo, enveloped in the lookout's emanations, came to inspect her at the end of mealtime and made such inventive funny faces at her that she laughed to the point of tears. Rolling backward, he disappeared, joyful, already elsewhere, while she wiped her eyes.

They had the patience of angels. Their tools attested to it. The ant twig, drinking sponge, digging stick, hollow suctioning stalk, and the honey dipper were slow, not very productive resources, rarely conserving energy. Their gourmandise could make them lose more calories than it offered them. Duane had seen Abbi spend hours fishing for tiny larva in some rotten wood to obtain the equivalent of a half-fistful of smooth rice. But these little predations were not only a matter of taste. If they rolled up certain roots at the edge of evaporated puddles to cover them in mineral salts, licking them off their fingers, it was also for their beneficial qualities. Formic acid brought out the flavor of mango leaves at the end of the season and promoted digestion. It was also an active antiparasitic. Duane had seen the lookout, afflicted with alopecia in his flank and buttocks, sit down in a carefully chosen and kneaded mud. They took care of themselves and each other.

Food, movement, and groome had flowed into the world like a river into its bed. Without friction, without any loss, without anything that was useful or anything that was useless.

They did not injure themselves or each other.

From watching them, Duane had learned how to hold her head. The semi-circular canal of her inner ear was now on a horizontal plane. She mastered the technique of squatting, of sitting, she knew how to lean forward while bending at the knees and haunches, she knew how to get back up, to dig in the soil and pluck things out of the air while holding her head in the axis of her neck, her nape upright. The form of her body had been subtly transformed. Her field of consciousness, and the objects to which she was attached, had nothing to do with what it could have been. Journeying through the corridors and traversing patches sharpened her senses and concentrated her needs. Hunger made her discover unexpected sources of food, fear made her react with increased speed. Silence oppressed her and reduced her to tiny dimensions. She perceived herself as powerful and capable of action, in a permanent state of wakefulness, poised on the edge of a sharp blade.

Since her admission into the society of Eips, she had developed a knowledge of the primitive body, the extent of its complexity surprising her day after day. Through paying attention to others, to their slightest gesture, postural choices, vocal manifestations, through imitation, indirectly, she had dug into her muscles and genes, into the loam of a very old memory. She had found there a knowledge that was a practice, she had found that all knowledge can only be a practice. There are a hundred ways to eat wild celery. There is only one way and the Eips had taught it to her.

She had been following them for so long that she was beginning to understand their idea of territory. Or rather, that to apply the concept of territory to their displacements was an aberration. The expanse didn't surround them, didn't concern them. They were regularly in front of such and such thicket, such and such ant hive, such and such row of bushes, such and such inlet, when they needed to be, when the thicket produced its fruits, when they were thirsty, when they needed antiseptic, when they wanted sugar or the soft nests that the trees provided in certain precise places, but each known position, taken up in the flux, was fresh, integrated instantly, implicated once again in the net of their practice. Not recognized but considered for what it was in its strict currentness. Duane saw them approach a huge landslide as if it had always been there, between a pond and two hectares of frequently traversed copses. She remained speechless before the mass of rubble, the magnitude of piled up and destroyed tree trunks at the foot of the cliff, cut out as if from a massive blow with a spade. She moved to the very edge of the cut, on top of the bulging earth from which ripped up roots emerged. She listened to the stones displaced by her approach bounce and roll against the vertical face down to the bottom of the hole—long seconds. And at the very bottom, she saw Gwongo balance on top of a platform six meters tall. The rapidity of the adaptation they showed had nothing in common with her own.

Duane had a thousand hypotheses about the

cause of such plasticity. No matter what she did to keep herself from doing so, her mind fell back into the structures and ruts of reason. She wandered in her search for answers, often finding no solace in the multitude of her questions save when one or another of the Eips made a sound at her that brought her back to the heart of the group—neither burdened with nor detached from the world.

Then Adda pushed her.

They were on top of a rocky slab, all sitting or semi-stretched out on the warm skin of ancient granite, blinking and watching the light play through the leaves of the trees that grew there and seemed to stretch out in the fading light. They paid attention to the lapping of the river twenty meters beneath them, to the sound of insects running on the wood, they groomed themselves with little irregular grunts—calm, settled into inaction, perhaps even into voluptuousness.

Duane was lying flat on her belly next to Gwongo on the rock. She tried to feel where, inside her body, the stone's heat in her viscera met that of the sun on her back. A zone was beginning to take shape, orange, floating, as thin as a blade of grass. When the universe was torn apart. She was upright in the blink of an eye, lifted up by the backs of her knees, clinging to the compact rock between the abyss of the sky and the abyss of the water. The lookout cried out, Adda threw her into the void with a single push. And the event of her fall took place. Built on the curve of the momentum that was received and absorbed, grazed, guided, tethered to the groomes hurled in her general direction, touched in a thousand places by the movement—future, past, present—cradled like a child swaddled in a blanket that became lighter, more floating, more absorbent as she fell, immediately settling bit by bit into a constant, unmoving velocity, knowing all of a sudden how to thread everything together, to stretch out her arms, engage her body, carry her head, neck aligned with the back, hands joined in front of her—how to take the plunge.

Ricochets

It had touched the surface at the ideal twenty-degree angle. Stabilized by its centrifugal movement, it dug a cavity into the fluid determined by its speed of rotation and translation combined with the water's viscous resistance and inertial force. It maintained its angle of attack forty-one times in a row until the parameters of impact reached the lower limit beneath which it could only surf, then succumb to gravity and sink.

Forty-one skips!

Garwan leaped from slab to slab to retrieve his stone. He was fired up. He had just beat the last known record for skipping stones and confirmed, through duly recorded experiments, his calculations concerning the variation of the horizontal component of velocity. He laughed openly, plunging his hand into the cool water to seize the stone he had spent entire evenings polishing. His favorite, gray and smooth, barely veined with white, smooth to the touch, warm like skin.

He had gotten it by battling it out during the end-of-year festivities. What he held in the palm of his hand was a pretty trophy, a stone that was local to the region, nearly intact, polished by an authentic terrestrial flood, a shard of legend, a *trupebble*. He had handled it so often that his fingers positioned themselves instinctively around the rounded edge, the first phalanx of his index finger against the miniscule notch that, like a trigger, was used to imprint the gyratory movement, the arc of the thumb hugging the pebble's body but remaining flexible, ready to let go at the strongest point of the momentum sent from shoulder to forearm to wrist.

For Garwan, skipping was an art. A branch of applied physics that he liked, but, above all, an art. The number of variables was so large that you needed a brain and a body with a particularly developed sense of finesse to even try to do it. But you needed above all the intimate perception of the moment, absolutely present, when the stone *needed* to leave the hand and take flight.

The axis, eccentric force, and power were variables that could be acquired and taught, but that decisive intuition, which you either had or didn't, was the incalculable inspiration, the spark that transformed technique into talent. And Garwan had just experienced it. It had gone through his head and arm like a flash of lightning, a euphoric sensation. He hoped there would be a trace of it in the reference chronofilms, one way or another.

Still skipping, he went back up the slab pathway, shaking his soaked sleeve to spray the water as far away as possible from him, he was ten years old, he felt like his legs were those of a deer or a wasp, he was no longer entirely certain.

The room had returned to stillness since the ripples and circles he had provoked with his magic pebble had been sucked up into the pond's denseness. Bathed in a zenithal light verging on yellow, devoid of any object beside the slabs that led to the end of the waterway, it was intended for horizontality and, for several hours each day, for the shrubby meditation he practiced from time to time.

On Ostiah, education occurred according to the tastes and interests of each learner. Garwan was pretty versatile. He avoided contact sports and games organized around nets and hoops, but he could run endlessly after a similibutterflye or a material idea thrown at top speed onto the field of large slides. He also liked anything to do with ballistics and lift, and not necessarily in a smaller form. However, his deep passion, from his earliest memory on, was for animates.

He gathered his jacket and checked the session's recording. The images played in slow motion on his tablette. He was happy enough with it to save viewing the holo for later, maybe in his personal square, maybe in the screening room, he'd think about it.

He called his drakitten, which leapt immediately into his shoulder pocket, and crossed the slider without a thought for the last drops of water that were rolling down the glass walls. He wasn't in a hurry, but the subtle electricity of his throw had given him an idea. He found himself almost immediately in front of the door to the great greenhouses.

Tuli opened his nostrils before they'd even entered into the humid dome filled with the smells of humus, plasma, and open flowers. He was an extremely reactive drakitten. He changed colors as soon as they'd passed by the tray of augmented ficuses and the vivarium full of kin. As was his habit, he didn't look over at the creatures crawling among the shiny leaves of this piece of jungle smothered in steam. Garwan wasn't proud of Tuli's attitude, but the drakitten turned his head away in such an ostentatious and showy manner that it made him smile on the inside. He flicked Tuli's tail through his pocket. On Ostiah, it was bad manners to be contemptuous. You could say whatever you wanted, but you could not reject anything on the basis of form or color. All creations were related and all were equally, even if not identically, alive. Just as there was no reason to deny the qualifier *living* to a chemical if it brought together the four determining characteristics, there was no reason to find repulsive a brown, spumy moss that devoured plankton and moved two centimeters per decan like an excremental plastic bag at the bottom of an ocean. It wasn't responsible for the troubling images and associations it provoked in reptilian brains. Certain forms of filiation were, perhaps, not the most agreeable, but what individual could boast of celebrating their family's actions and family resemblances in their integrality?

The charged air of the greenhouse made Garwan's lungs rejoice. He walked, taking big steps and greeting those he crossed with a ritual abridged gesture that protected him from being interrupted in his progress. He stopped before the germination tray that he'd reserved six weeks ago and studied it. The snapdragonesses were budding. Their tiny fuzzy triangular heads were pointing up out of the green coat lined with mauve silk. There were six or seven to each fragile ridge, drenched in liquid nutrients, visibly in good shape.

Garwan leaned over the tray and stuck his mouth to the hygiaphone to speak to them. He didn't say any old thing just to produce the waves they needed—he gave articulate speeches, tested out rhetorical forms and a variety of narrative genres. Sometimes, he would also simply recount his dreams or offer up an algebraic problem he was occupied by at that moment. This time, he sang a very simple little couplet, a nursery rhyme that he didn't know he remembered, and watched them orient themselves toward his voice. The little blind faces, bundled up in their pods, inflated their pelts and trembled, lulled by the rhythm and the child's warm breath as if by a breeze as warm and humid as they could wish for. Their reactions to the sounds were increasingly visible. Garwan no longer needed an eyepiece to examine them, and that was also a euphoric sensation. To examine with the naked eye. With no other instrument than his senses, no tool for stimulating them other than his vocal cords.

Through the walls of the germination block, they were now nearly at the point of being able to establish a body-to-body relation. He repeated the song while watching them oscillate and vibrate up and down the length of their stalks. It was a general movement, the maws at the top of the stalk took advantage of the momentum of the others to accentuate the slack, the amplitude was increasing, identical across all the ridges, down to the micron, Garwan could have bet on it. He was accompanying the little maws' dancing without knowing it, swaying above the hygiaphone as if the song that he thought he was uttering, that was taking them over, had enveloped him as well. He lost himself in the exchange that was taking place without needing to take initiative, and the harmony was true, sweet, very tranquil. The spell was broken when Tuli gave him three warning taps on his shoulder. His adhesive pads, as small as they were, could take on the quality of a mosquito bite. Garwan gave him another flick and unstuck his mouth from the hygiaphone. Nimbly, Tuli pointed out one of the mouths at the top with his tongue. Garwan leaned over and witnessed what he'd been waiting for so impatiently since he had sown the seeds. The snapdragoness, more than halfway out of its coat, turned its head from left to right and right to left to get rid of the rest of its birthing husk, and before its closed eyes—two silky bulges on either side of the cranial ridge—could even appear, Garwan made out the profile of its jaw, the tiny wicker fold that still sealed the teeth inside their pink cavity, then, just before the blooming, before the opening of the ocular globes and the unfolding of the ears, he saw what he was dying to see—its first voluntary movement, the first comer, its smile. Naïve, predatory, indolent. A shock.

As soon as the first head was out, the stalks were overcome with somersaults—all the faces at the top and along the stalks wanted to come out at the same time. There was a frenetic wriggling, husks raining down, then, suddenly, calm came over the thin shrub, who no longer did anything but blink with all its brand-new eyes and its opened and reclosed maws.

The drakitten was like a stone on the boy's shoulder. His claws, which rarely came out, had gripped onto the fabric of his jacket tightly enough to form balls that he was firmly attached to. He had become a statue, his eyes open, absolutely still. Garwan's gaze, on the contrary, moved from stalk to stalk and head to head with the speed of lightning. He didn't want to miss any of the tiny differences that distinguished them from each other—the color of the eyes, the implantation of the hairs, the position of the skull, the forelock of one, the purplish-blue tongue of another—he wanted to perceive the slightest variation at the very moment it appeared in order to be able to name it as quickly as possible. Violette, The Cornlick, The Beard, Baby Potato, Odd-Eye, Pear,

Pointy, Chitchat, Foria, Maxym—he named ten of them and changed his mode of perception. Not focusing his eyes but letting them dilate little by little until he obtained an attentive and floating view of the whole. In this full, weightless cloud, without any intention or any given direction, he contemplated the formation as it was. It wasn't the sum of individuals, a group, but a whole, an organism endowed with eighteen not at all smooth brains. And eighteen gaping, famished maws.

Garwan turned on his heels and left to get food. He fed them with flakes of dried, deep-sea-shrimp-flavored seitan. The nutrient closet was full of mixtures, the production of which he'd participated in, but the mineral protein powder he'd concocted was long gone. Into which digestive tubes, he couldn't say. On Ostiah, you helped yourself to the available reserves. You tried foodstuffs in case they were suitable for the targeted body. His powder had perhaps nourished the wheat from which the seitan he was now using came, because nothing disappeared in the world.

When he had finished the distribution, which had taken on the appearance of a brief snowstorm, the little maws closed simultaneously. He saw another smile stretch out their jawbones, a flash in eighteen pairs of eyes followed by a reflexive movement of the muzzles toward the stalks and toward what remained of a downy swelling at the base of the originary husk. They fell asleep. The drakitten reawakened only once they had confirmed that a deep snoring had taken over the tray. He threw his rolled tongue into the box of seitan that Garwan hadn't closed yet and swallowed a good amount. The child shook his head, put the lid back on and took his companion's favorite sweet out of his back pocket. A shrunken fruit fly that tasted like a charnel house. Tuli licked his nostrils for several long minutes after ingesting it so quickly that Garwan might well have doubted he'd held the stinking miniature fly between his fingers had he not given up on apprehending the drakittens' swift predation with his human senses. To satisfy his curiosity, he'd once stroboscopically filmed one of Tuli's meals and come to understand why no creature could escape capture, even if it were endowed with a radar and an eye with thirty-six facets: even slowed down, it was nearly impossible to decompose the movement. Tuli was at point A, the fly at point B, his tongue came out, went back in maybe, then the fly was no longer at point B. He needed to push the calibration to the max to be able to truly see the action take place. The safest thing is to either not be a fly in Tuli's presence, or to be a fly much too large for him.

While going to put the box of seitan back in the closet, Garwan crossed paths with Siand, who looked like he was looking for something. Siand was small for his age, stocky and very emotional. His naturally yellow complexion had turned, he was almost phosphorescent in the charged atmosphere of the greenhouse, and he smelled acidic. Siand was clearly in the middle of producing a COVB characteristic of stress, but Garwan was able to tolerate the body odors of others without problem, even those which were negative. He had learned, like everyone else on Ostiah, that there is no odor that is bad in and of itself. The hyrax's petrified urine, for instance, combined with opoponax, with dead, tanned skin and with a molecule of agaric, resulted in something that whet the appetite of all known omnivores. He gave the ritual greeting and asked the agitated kid in front of him, three months his junior, what was wrong.

Siand had just lost his last lot of honeysuckle, not one of the promising young shoots had passed the stage of the fourth foliole—he was despondent. He had read and reread the treatises, he had verified the hygrometry and phosphate levels every day at the set time, he had moved the lamps by the book, cycling appropriately, but the litter had withered barely emerged from the soil. The saddest part, he said, was precisely that they had made it out of the earth. If the seeds hadn't transformed, if they had remained deaf to the call of the light, the call of growth, he would have been consoled, but it was failing at the very beginning, at the initial decision, that most powerful and tender moment, which disturbed him. It was frustrating, a hope vanished, time and attention lost, but, beyond the objective disappointment, it was sad. Garwan knew this feeling, he had also tried cuttings and seedlings that hadn't taken, or that had atrophied without his understanding the reason. He tried to comfort Siand by quoting one of the founding adages of Ostiah: "Modest in hope and in defeat," but the other was already too yellow to make do with so little. He shrugged his shoulders and declared in a trembling voice that he would try to remember the next time, even if a modest hope seemed to him to be a perfect oxymoron. "Hope is mad or it is not at all," he added before turning his back on him and heading toward the Tropics section of the greenhouse. Garwan couldn't stop himself from noticing that the yellow of his skin had, nonetheless, returned to a warmer shade.

Hope didn't have to be mad. It was a sign of *hybris* to think such a thing—now, everyone on Ostiah knew where excess led, but they also knew that you need to let creatures think and carry out their experiments.

Honeysuckle growing was a classic for ninth-years, there wasn't anything outrageous about it. Things failed as often as they succeeded—Siand's problem lay not in the seed nor in the soil. He was sentimental, thought Garwan, looking at the immense laterals of a camphor tree three rods high—like us all.

He always visited the *Dipterocarpaceae* alveolus when he passed by. It was full to bursting, stuffed with green from the ground to the ceiling, breathing. Density was optimal. The large leaves stretched their extremities toward the neighboring tree as if to touch it and in a movement of desire mixed with restraint, changed their mind before making contact. The crowns were close to each other, as close as possible, but they didn't touch. In all circumstances and even in strong winds, there were always twenty centimeters of air free between each crown and when you stretched out at their feet or on the glass plane of the ceiling, the sight was graphic, it evoked tectonic plates and their waltzing drift, but one couldn't say if the dynamic was one of separation or of reunion. Garwan often increased the speed of gaseous displacement to confirm once again, each time, that strong to very strong agitations didn't change anything about the phenomenon. The leaves blew, the branches bent, the pompoms swayed every which way—despite the turning and the twisting that could be imparted to the air currents by positioning the fans, they danced together and never stepped on each other's heads. Like the clustered inflorescences of cauliflower, but free and green in the movements that started with a shared trunk, the spheres of leaves keeping distance while seeming to do away with it. Garwan felt that there was something erotic about it without knowing exactly what.

He had an aerial idea of sexuality, based on a number of observations of real situations and on typologies of perpetuation that were very different from each other. He also knew that reproduction wasn't his primary function, nor, for that matter, was production. He himself had had relations of varying degrees of sensuality with his plantings, the animates, his familiar aliens and his different kin. For example, sharing the results of his recent stone skipping session with Gowind, whose experiences and springy gait he admired, was going to be a satisfying moment of excitement, he could look forward to it. He would move on later, perhaps, to specifically carnal caresses, but both of them knew that they were already in a relationship and a physico-chemical exchange that was, in sexual terms, advanced. He wondered sometimes what their amorous acts would give rise to, what kind of effects they would produce in them and in the world, in what way they would manifest.

They didn't have the creative power of plants, they were humans, but their ambitus wasn't nothing, and Garwan was devoured, in sudden and uncontrolled fits, by curiosity regarding this matter.

Desire created form and function. Nobody knew which primitive *Amborella*, tired of being caressed solely by the wind, had invented the bee as sexual extension. Nobody thought much about it on Ostiah, as origins meant hardly anything, all life forms being a variation of each other, poorly or well replicated. After this innovation, or contemporaneously, others had developed insects with plunging tubes, insects with claws, insects with hairy, grippy, irritating legs, little rodents with fur, gentle and furtive, grazing bats thirsty for nectar, persistent, powdery butterflies well equipped with uncoiling trunks. There was something for all corollas—small, deep, splayed, hooded, radiating out—for all colors, all juices, and all pollens.

The diversity of sexual organs born from the desire of plants was astounding. Their erotic inventiveness had engendered the complexity of the world. Its forms and its entanglement. The orangutang and bombyx were nothing other than two pornographic reveries shared by an arboreal body that easily managed to grow itself through cuttings and layering, but, out of a taste for play and amorous display, held on to these indiscreet jewels with their supple and firm forms.

The animates' mobility must be the butt of plants' jokes, Garwan thought. The detours, surges, hesitations, the free will that mammals—humans included—and others—birds—prided themselves on were certainly part of the green lineage's lovers' discourse. Garwan didn't believe in detail as determinism, nor did he feel diminished. His imagination was stimulated by that of others. An overflowing fantasy couldn't, in any case, constitute an obstacle for a self-possessed mind. Taken up in this continuous creation, he was also capable of taking up. Of singing a lullaby to eighteen very much alive snapdragonesses, of embracing, through little leaps, the surface of a pond, covering it before sliding on it, soaked, compact, already overflowing, and plunging into it with pleasure.

He had heard talk of the impoverishment of the sexual experiences allowed for between hominids on the source planet. He had been stupefied by it and hadn't ceased questioning the teach-er responsible for the module until he threw in the towel, telling Garwan that the ritual mores of ancient societies had nothing to do with any actual reality. He had attempted to explain to him that the construction of a norm could be based on a distorted or simplified interpretation of the environment and of co-living beings, that it was, at bottom, the prerequisite for the formation of a norm, but Garwan hadn't understood. He didn't understand either the causes or the use. At no level, individual or collective, did the reduction of desires and the means of satisfying them seem advantageous, and the strategy of avoiding vari-ables, power factors, seemed to him to lead first to frustration, then to the flattening of creative facul-ties. That a form of power could be linked to this program of depletion generated a sense of mal-aise in him that he couldn't manage to pin down completely. The *hominina* and the *homo* with their big brains hadn't displayed any great intelligence during the last phase of their terrestrial history and Garwan was undoubtedly still looking for external causes for their demise, occasionally finding some, but, when he revisited this aspect of their rules for living, he faltered. This obstacle stopped him like a wall too lengthy to be gone around, too thick to be pierced.

The teach-er had advised him to set aside this ancillary study. He reminded him that not all difficulties were real problems and that one could side-step a mystery when the world was vast. And Ostiah was huge. Launched into a continuously expanding space, opening onto the outside through thousands of doors, windows, and airlocks, she navigated through empty space in proximity to an infinite number of celestial objects, herself carrying an infinite number of life forms in the process of becoming—a world among other worlds. She was pretty and inhabited, definitely alive, to be nurtured and cultivated, like a mind and a seed.

Garwan left the *Dipterocarpaceae* alveolus with satisfied nostrils, a smile on his lips. He felt like getting a good cradling in the fruit of *Ceiba pentandra* mapou wouj, which held the axis of Ostiah somewhere in its folds and buttresses bristling with spikes. Garwan knew how to advance along the length of the shaft by using the spines as steps. The woolly monkeys had taught him to flow through the holds and the rests in such a way that he could grab the edges without being cut by these rapiers. He would reach the first horizontals in less than twenty breaths without a single scratch. Past the defensive zone, the tree's tenderness was supreme. The wrinkles of the bark at the branch crotch were smooth on the hands and feet. One climbed up it with every available limb, hugging the trunk as much as possible. Garwan's arm couldn't go around even the smallest branch, he could lie down, open his legs, and stretch out without reaching the edge of the branches. He ran there like he did at the large slides, without looking at the ground, he flew through the leaves.

Arriving at the foot of the Great Tree, the drakitten immediately took the lead on the climb. Garwan followed, dynamic and poised, because whatever anyone says, ten years puts you at the threshold of maturity. He explored the medians while looking at the epiphyte colonies with interest. The paths of orchids, the squares of pendulous ferns, the moss hangings, the begonia beds, everything that contributed to making up the hanging garden attached to mapou wouj axis mundi, without ever removing anything to its detriment. Certain small frogs with dorsal bubbles thus chose to be tree-dwelling and no longer descended, neither to drink nor to lay eggs, preferring to use for these two vital activities the open cups of bromeliads that they had gotten to know. These organisms shared the charm of being both guests and hosts, as well as the knowledge of the tightrope walker, which kept them to the line of the ridge, neither parasites nor parasitized.

Next to them, Garwan was a passerby, an apprentice of the periphery, a come-and-goer whose center of gravity wasn't fixed. He stepped as lightly as he could and attempted to open his ear to the wadding that surrounded him. He looked for a capsule his size, split at the top, which wouldn't mind welcoming him. He called Tuli, who was on him in three leaps, his crest adorned with a black and dark blue geometric motif inspired by an amphibian he had just crossed paths with. Garwan whistled admiringly. The drakitten blushed all the way down to his neck. He asked him to start searching. Tuli jumped on top of his head, then in front of him, then shot off like an arrow toward the tufts of leaves on the delicate branches, which he used as catapults. He was soon ten stories above Garwan, and after one of his famous strikes with his multidirectional eye, he tapped out the spatial coordinates of a pod that seemed to do the trick.

It was a still green bivalve, long and narrow, plump, ready to open. Garwan approached it cautiously. He knocked three times on the hanging pod, waited. A creaking could be heard, very similar to the sound produced by an imago leaving its old skin. The bean cracked open, showing its white, spongy, silky lining, the thick cotton of its dispersal parachute still compressed into the smallest space possible, and, soon, a black ball spurted out of its belly, then another, then a hundred, and Garwan slid into the space that they had emptied out, into the middle of the satiny, warm material. He stood up in the deserted fruit, enveloped so closely that he didn't have to make any effort at all, wrapped up in a cloud, more serene than a seed in an apple.

The drakitten remained across from him, his legs wrapped around the stalk. Garwan saw him

gaze at the top of the capsule with so much con-
centration that he understood what was soon to
follow. Tuli puffed up his chest, his muscles undu-
lated underneath his skin, his dorsal crest unfurled
from behind his head down to the end of his tail,
his nostrils dilated and contracted to an unusual
rhythm, he began hyperventilating, Garwan didn't
budge. Then, all of a sudden, with the devastating
speed that he was made of, Tuli opened up two red
wings trimmed with gold, crushed the peduncle of
the capsule, which gave way immediately, and took
the whole pod with Garwan inside it between his
two anterior legs, suddenly tiny under these sails.

The weight pulled them down toward the
ground, the drakitten curved its spine, veered to
the left, to the right, and found stability. Garwan
took flight, swollen, expanded, comfortable,
wrapped up, carried away by his pod, a mind and a
seed, a heart in a body. A destiny in space.

Uiush

Uiush was hung well.

He hadn't come down for ten days.

A great pyralid had come four times during sunrise and beaten her wings in front of his left eye.

Uiush knew her lineage. He could expect a fifth occurrence and prepare to shift his arm so as to move her out of the way with a meaningful movement, but she would probably try again, and maybe in front of his right eye, which would render all of his arrangements useless.

As is often the case, it was wiser to hold off on impulsive reactions.

If the great pyralid had come four times to swarm under his nose, it wasn't without a valid reason. Imperious.

The sun struck Uiush all along his left flank. He was satisfied with the posture he had chosen in the twilight, considering with care the position of the stars and the bearing of the wind. His predictions had been confirmed. He was, indeed, at the end of the branch of Cecropia, due east, camouflaged by the palm leaves around his head and bathed by the nascent heat of the still-red star that would soon turn yellow.

Uiush appreciated the sensation.

He shared it with his branch. They were there, the both of them, comfortable, thirty meters above ground, one half in the heat, the other half in the cool. It was a singular moment whose reoccurrence had to be calculated. Envisioned long before its appearance, it had been all the more delightful.

What the branch knew, the great pyralid, perhaps, did not. She was a perfect guest, the picture of discretion, exquisitely delicate in the diversity of her movements, which were nonetheless completely frenzied. She led her group by example with an exceptional lightness. There were more than a hundred twenty of them without counting the irregulars, whose presence was as light as nothing.

Uiush was housed well with his pyralids. He

didn't complain. Moths that his mother herself had nurtured? How could he complain? An alliance prepared well in advance. Certain males who no longer left save rarely ended up abandoning their wings in his fur. No one here was weighed down with useless organs. Uiush received this gift gratefully, knowing what kind of renunciation it meant for such a restless species, always so busy frolicking and playing around in his fur, from the top of his head to the end of his feet.

They groomed him with their dances. They barely tickled him since his hair was so dense and tough, enveloped in a green, erosion-resistant sheath. The pyralids were free to carry out their flirtations and sabbats on his back in peace, most of the time he didn't even notice. Or rather, the aeration they provided him with was part of his climate. He had integrated it as an element of thermoregulation. He offered protection, warmth, a portion of their food, they tended to his bowl cut and face makeup, this racoon mask to which he was so attached. They weren't satisfied with fanning him, they shook his fur as experienced hairdressers, promoting the growth of algae that provided him with the golden and green hues of which he was rather proud.

Uiush was stylish.

He considered the presence of a number of cyanobacteria and chlorophyllic symbiotes in his bodily finery to be of great benefit. It was, in his eyes, the sign and the definition of a choice fur. As well as the sign of his intimacy with the world. The greener and more iridescent he was, the more he was a leaf among leaves, hanging by his hardened claws onto his branch, in sync with his host's atmosphere. The tree carried him the way he carried his moths, beetles, algae, and sanitary viruses. Graciously. He was invested in not tickling it, in weighing no more than a loosely attached hammock, in never scuffing the bark. And above all, in never picking up speed.

Uiush hoped that he was more gifted by far than the moths in his coat. That, by way of his attention, he was able to melt into the tree's continuous movement. Day and night, Uiush sensed its growth, its ceaseless exercise, its organs multiplying, its absorption and transpiration, the rising up of its sap, its growth. Through adjacency, he heard the roots' vibration in relative fluidity underground.

Himself suspended, hanging on to the branch of the moment with twelve calcified peduncles, as motionless and as agitated as his wood was among the attached, spinning leaves, he felt the slightest movement of the air, the breeze, the storm and its reappearances, the way the gaseous material bathed and dabbed the folioles without letting up, and the tenacious activity of the body that was insinuating itself into his environment.

Uiush breathed oxygen at its source. Uiush ate the sun transformed by the still warm chloroplasts. Uiush drank the water of the sky, the dew, the sweat of the tree's underarms.

He scratched his chin when he had to. He blinked his eyes in moderation. He decided on each of his movements knowingly, in a state of compos mentis.

An ant climbing onto the trunk was not unfamiliar to him. Nor was the approach of an ocelot, of a band of monkeys on edge, or of an eight-kilo raptor with outsize tarsi.

He knew how to wait for them and surprise

them from the depths of his apparent inertia. They were too confident, these massive animals that were all muscles and reckless expenditure. Uiush didn't need to move more than a few vertebrae to follow the course of a nebulous panther. Be it from the sky, the ground, or the immediate horizon, he seized its presence and the cautiousness of its progress as soon as it put a paw on a tree that was connected to his own. By air or by ground, through resonance and deduction, he knew who was entering into the neighboring wood at the very moment of contact. Trusting the forest's report, he was able to predict the predator's type of approach and physiological state.

Uiush watched the ventral locomotion of neofelines with interest. The excessive weight of their bodies, the abruptness of their movements, the violent tremors they imparted to everything they touched, the downtime they observed, out of trickery or out of sudden exhaustion, their sensational about-faces, their barely cushioned falls—everything pointed to incoherence and a fragmentation of the will on the part of these dismantled beings. Even their coats were riddled with holes. The demonstrative motility of their shoulders, aberrant aesthetically and economically speaking, could send shivers down your spine from its excess.

The harpies were hardly better balanced. They hurtled from the canopy like hairy sandbags incapable of controlling their sails. Their limbs—legs, huge beak, tail, thick torso—impeded them, down to the feathers on their cap. They fell heavily onto the branches, getting tangled up in the twigs, looking blindly to grab onto anything and soon found themselves in the situation of someone drowning in three inches of water, beating their wings and their fingers to try to float in the panic they had provoked.

Uiush observed these scenes with a singular eye. It wasn't desirable to disturb an optimal position simply out of a contagious anxiety. Moreover, these rough interventions only rarely called for a perceptual change. The data they delivered, well before their actual irruption, were so numerous and so simple, that combat, or, more often, its simulacrum, would end in a draw, over before it had even begun.

It so happened, on several occasions, that he had to unhook three claws from his branch and suspend an anterior one in the air at the appropriate spot. A harpy had taken off, blinded in one eye, shrieking. An ocelot had run down the trunk like the long trail of blood it left behind, possessing, for once, a hint of elegance.

As for the monkeys, the red ones in particular, though they were tree-dwelling, they were considered by Uiush to be impostors. The less he saw of them, the better he felt. As a group, they were capable of shaking a tree's structure down to its most fragile rootlets while they leapt about without any goal in mind other than showing off their supposed dynamic talent and the exploits of a prehensile tail. Childish. Their rhythm was so stupid that Uiush would have preferred to sleep each time they showed up, but these chattering things were looking for trouble. They would come and pull on the hairs on his head, shove sticks in his ears, whistle to see if he was deaf—six or seven of them would get onto his branch and swing violently to see if he would fall.

Uiush had chosen his form and his path a long

time ago. He was green, absolutely green, devoted to plants, fluid like lava. He had nevertheless had to restrain himself *in extremis* from decapitating some of them with his saber-like backhand. Luckily, these imbeciles picked up on danger when it was nearby and potentially deadly. They wound up leaving him in peace. His most common mood, his only action. Peace, the foundation of his life.

Uiush decided to bring back up an already chewed leaf from his median stomach compartment. It had to be sufficiently softened for him to get to the soft stuff he needed. The mere thought of the red monkeys could shift his mood subtly, this was a tendency he had to controvert. Cecropia leaves weren't very nourishing, but Uiush knew how to prepare them in a way that increased their benefits tenfold. His preference was for simple food. Poor food, passed over by other mammals, uncompetitive, ill-suited for supplying the astronomical amounts of energy that most ambulatories required. Even the caterpillars turned away from his usual pasture. Uiush was pleased because these metamorphic parentheses, these little hooped sausages, always on the verge of splitting open from the internal pressure they inflicted on themselves, were big enough to be able to devastate an entire tree in a single night of work. They would leave behind veins pointing up toward the sky like fish bones and translucent lacework in the leaves that they hadn't devoured completely. After their passing through, a tree would have a hangdog, robbed, and exhausted look and, if its network was too damaged, it could take it months to rebuild. Uiush had witnessed one of these blitzkriegs. He had even had to change trees on this occasion and had suffered for it.

The secret was to carry out digestion at the stage it was in. Bringing back a leaf that had been macerating since it was swallowed a few days earlier was a way to guarantee immediate comfort. The stomachal infusion induced a light fermentation that bestowed a natural relaxation. Uiush didn't overdo it and made good use of his four digestive compartments. The rotation that he'd developed was a model of measured renewal. He did not gobble heaps of food. He removed a slice of chloroplast here and there, making sure his extractions were spaced out, no more than three on the same end, no more than six on the same branch, no more than a dozen per bough. Besides, generally speaking, he was full once he reached the fourth, as his gastric pouch couldn't contain much more.

Harvesting was an intense activity. Apart from choosing the piece based off where it was on the twig, he had to pay attention to its exposure, which determined its degree of maturation, and to its temperature. A leaf that was too cold could end up being difficult to dissolve, a leaf that was too warm could provoke the growth of indigenous yeasts that were likely to block the eupeptic properties of his intestinal flora. At bottom, the secret to a good feeding lay in mastication. It had to be done without haste, at the end of a delicate harvest, and had to mobilize all of his teeth. Uiush had only molars in his mouth. He wouldn't have known what to do with a pair of canines or sharp incisors. His system was as effective as a millstone; with the right technique, he was able to produce a vegetal paste that was of a homogenous consistency, gentle on the palate going down and coming back up.

The third stage of the bolus was the smoothest. The alcohol effluvia had melted, present but almost indiscernible, and the warm mush thus had a spirituous effect. It loosened him up. He entered into a direct relation with chlorophyl in the form that he was able to assimilate, with the solar rays that the little green limbs had held onto and stored up day after day. He disintegrated and reintegrated this astral power on which the earth depended, he gorged himself on edible light. Like the tree—his host, his support—he pushed his body into space while feeding on electromagnetic waves, he slid into the atmosphere while absorbing it, he touched the heart of his movement.

The beating of his heart, the bellows of his lungs, the involuntary play of his muscle fiber were tied to this minuscule transmission that built him up, leaf after leaf.

Uiush lived not off wind, but off light. He had chosen his side, he didn't put his weight down.

While chewing his thoughts over, he felt heat turning around his branch. The sun had risen at the same time as his blood sugar, day had broken.

Through the palm leaves that covered him, he followed the loony flight of a toco toucan preceded by the yellow mass of its beak daubed with black.

The bird passed by, rowing, resting on its breast, stretched out. It alternated between rapid beating and a diving glide that was horrendously brief. It sunk with each beat of a wing and weighed on the air, which supported its movements to the point of giving it a few seconds of a horizontal glide before letting it fall again, the other slapping back what had been peacefully offered up. Uiush was no longer surprised by the endless negotiations that the ambulatories engaged in with their support. Both parties were undoubtedly satisfied with them. The atmosphere was stirred up by flight, perhaps itching deliciously at the caress of feathers, and, for its part, the bird, crossing all over, simultaneously inflating and sinking through its element, found a sensation of intermittent equilibrium that suited it.

Uiush blinked his eyes while swallowing, for the last time, his ball of ground greenery. Nothing he saw or felt, perceived one way or another, had the power to destroy his ataraxia.

Relaxed, Uiush was pinned onto his branch.

Most of the time, he confronted the world upside down, or at least what was upside down for the vast majority. But that didn't mean much since his nine vertebrae allowed him to swivel his head 270 degrees, just like his hypermobile joints, which enabled him to grab what was in front of him from a great multiplicity of angles. Flexibility and consistency were the abscissa and ordinate of his evolution.

Every one of his movements were like a trunk with its leaves and roots—of an intensity that evaded the perception of curious quadrupeds or bipeds. A falcon eye or a pair of binoculars wasn't enough to spot him. Uiush wore his cloak of invisibility like a trophy, the only one he'd ever sought to obtain. From the ground, he looked like a termite nest, a pile of stacked leaves. From the sky, he didn't exist, or was maybe a canker at the crossing of two tired branches.

The masks on foot who hunted in the forest spent hours whistling toward the treetops, trying to locate him. When he was in the mood, he turned his head completely and shot off a smile that made them scamper off in all directions. That amused him. A mask couldn't handle finding him. When one of them had discovered him, it immediately closed its eyes and produced sounds with its mouth to alert its peers, and when they were gathered under the tree, it was impossible for the one who'd made the alert to get remotely close to pointing out the right direction. At that point, Uiush's smile would be the largest in the world. And if he wanted to take the game further, all he needed to do was to send out his sharp cry three or four times—"ai, ai"—to then witness the most chaotic stampede. The masks on foot would go raving mad. Like other ambulatories, they had chosen ostentatiousness. They believed in size, in speed—in being the speediest—in a frontality without a behind. The bluer their masks, the madder they were.

Uiush's ancestors had steadily shrunk. They applied themselves successively, over the course of ten thousand years, to reducing their volume, strength, weight, the whole of their metabolism, appetite, and output. After the crisis in growth that had led them to weigh three hundred eighty kilos at three meters long, to rumble like caverns and shit out mountains, they had flipped it all. After Uñushi copulated with the Sun for three whole days, then the Moon right after; after they fell out in a bad way. In those days when mediation was no longer possible, when messengers came back burned up or frozen to the bone, birds plucked, anteaters hung by their tongues, cats declawed. When the star, the satellite, and the planet ran through the skies looking for each other to clear the air, Uñushi had gathered together his descendants from the Moon and the Sun alike—the jar, the tapir, the aquatic bird, and the spirit of the deep waters, and he said to them: I'm going to defecate here for one last time, a seed is in my feces, which will grow. Wait for it to reach the Moon, to reach the Sun, and when it will have spoken, cut the trunk and each of you is to go your own way. Then Uñushi immediately crouched down, shed three quarters of his weight, the seed emerged from his dung, grew at the top and at the bottom, and Uñushi climbed. His descendants could no longer see him. He reached the Moon, he reached the Sun, and he let out his cry. Then, in the darkest of night, the jar, tapir, aquatic bird, and spirit of the deep waters took turns with the saw cutting down the enormous trunk. They kicked at the trunk that had been separated from its roots, but the tree did not fall. It remained suspended in the canopy of heaven. A cousin undertook the journey and discovered that it was being held up by a tiny Uñushi using three fingers.

The large Uius who remained set off for the cemetery of the huge. They traversed the continent from the south to the north and from the east to the west in order to meet up with the hole of brown lava that was digesting the extra-large ones. Some of them reached it in their first form and dove in with the mammoths, the saber-toothed tigers, the dangerous wolves, the red eagles, the bison and the megaroaches to witness the existence of giants in their diversity. The majority of them, however, began to shrink on the way, and those who climbed the Californian palm trees weighed less than three pounds more than Uñushi, pinned onto the mythic baobab.

Since then, without avoiding each other, the Earth, Moon, and Sun keep a good distance, and the forests continue.

At the cost of immense fatigue, Uiush kept up the neighboring wood's network all by himself, it covered the hill from the river at the bottom all the way up to the top. He pinned leaves on the changing sky just with his claws poised between ether and bark, nearly seamless.

By becoming lighter, the Uius had left gravity. Their center of gravity was loose, adjusted to the continual lifting. Encouraged, the trees had specialized in the construction of arbors and of mezzanines. Host and guest alike inspired each other to treat the ground like a variety of air. With or without roots, they were the tie, the link, the tenuous thread—volatile, the slippage between two states of matter.

When he had reached this point, his lungs inflated with a breath taken with the necessary care, the great pyralid, as he'd expected, returned for the fifth time before his left eye, and Uiush understood that she wouldn't let him drag things out.

He let out a long, careful sigh and decided to surrender to the ritual. He reduced his power, removing one of his three claws, then two, then all of them, and indulgently began curbing his fall.

At more or less regular intervals, he had to feed the memory of his ancestors. As well as the humus at the feet of his host, the hub of his wood, the eggs of the pyralids raised by his own mother, and his algae, which were not averse to the change of scenery that came with the occasional terrestrial trip.

Uiush needed to descend, to take himself down, to unsuspend himself, and to shit on the ground in the most uncomfortable position so as to maintain the orbit of the three celestial objects with a rocky past.

In Deep

Storms are commonplace at the Border. You don't expect them; they're simply there, capricious and constant. Not a season passes, however, without an unexpected, inexplicable lull, which leaves the forest suddenly muted, the thalli hanging against the stems, the floats unmoving, three-quarters visible. The surface is heavy with its full weight and spreads its phantomlike threat down the stalks to the rocks, to the sand. It works its way into the caverns, penetrates the faults, stretches out over the depths, and subjects all of the guilds to a terrifying tranquility.

Each is thus found in the original jelly, brought to its limits, stripped of tricks for moving, taking up only as much space as its own body, without growth or power. Gills open and close slowly, eyes blink in slow-motion, cleaving or congealing, a dorsal fin undulates discreetly, a mouth shuts, an arm is set down. The entire forest holds its breath.

The canopy has fallen silent, nothing filters from up top. The brown, lifeless algae no longer transmit anything but the luminous wave in its simplest form, and the essence of what it knows how to do—penetrate, bathe, invade—it does in one go, without a distinctive glow, without a single captivating maneuver, an ounce of seduction. It's a sovereign force that establishes itself everywhere, completely, against which no resistance can be offered up. A force that presses and spins around an incommensurable axle, whose one direction and strictly fixed velocity leave nothing in the shadows.

During these formidable respites, all living things can take each other in down to the finest detail—deep inside their hiding places, their shells, their grottos, their fissures, in the heart of the column, in the flow of the surface, wherever they are, they sparkle, unveiled. Crude and nude in their skin, momentarily idle, with their eyes, they see in their forms the singular function for which they are destined. Like arrows suspended in suddenly compressed matter, they see, through each member of the world, the impersonal responsibility shared by all, the inescapable task of being, above all else, vectors of biomass.

Some transparent bodies with protruding eye sockets display it clearly throughout their life—the veiled jellyfish, the superlucid shrimp, the segments of silicone, laden with not very many antennae, a bit of gauze, some basic makeup, white trim, a mottled eyelid, tail feathering—and in the heart of primordial violence, travel exposed, apparently unarmed.

In these moments of absolute calm, large predators do not escape from the fact that they are an integral part of something that feeds and swallows them in the same movement. They are included and continually digested. A cruising pajama shark can implode under this unexpected pressure. In the usual turbulence, it will pass by all the currents, it will play in the most agitated water mass, it will reel in the gusts, happy with gliding, with its cutaneous corset, its sense of smell, but in the sticky stuff, stationary, its gills close, its brain curdles, a bubble gets stuck in its armor, and it bursts.

When the inert force embraces the forest down to its sandy floor, and the living things recognize each other for what they are, stupor strikes, there is no event, they remain where they were, in the center—multiple facets of a great ball of objective life, like so many little mirrors, they shine. The space fills up with reflections and indestructible silver. No body, in these conditions, finds the audacity to evolve. But if the moment drags on, and it does, one lone animal, among all the rest, will respond to it. Without lifting a single sucker, by using its knowledge, absorbing the force of its chromatophores, orienting its reflectors, modulating their brightness, it will change state in fractions of a second and outfit the ocean with a long chain of successive metamorphoses. Spiky, horned, brown, covered with cutting denticles, a rock suddenly dissolved in a flexible puddle, crushed on the ground, sticky, absorbed by the mottled sand, imperceptible, reappearing immediately as a star with spread out branches, striped with black and white, geometric, two arms gone, the others shaken by colorful flashes, luminescent, quick, pumped out, then smooth, flat, dull, summed up in three independent threads, forgotten and digressive, before recovering its head—an enormous balloon, a yellow siphon, two lateral eyes—and springing up like a flash in a black summer sky, tangling its net with a cloud of unstable pseudo-forms.

The storm doesn't need to pick up again, it's passed. The sideration has left the bodies, they've gotten their reflexes and appetites back, electrified by the demonstration. The octopus is hidden. The octopus has opened up like an umbrella, closed itself in on a crab whose carapace it's crushing, its beak is hard, the octopus has glided across the floor, attached itself, dug itself into the burrow, wrapped itself up in the grass, its body is liquid, the octopus has vanished.

Rhif hopes to see one each time he ascends to the Border. They fascinate him. The ones in the subsuperficial zone are the most attractive ones in his opinion. Their skills, illusionist technique, and combativity impressed him. If, on his part, he managed to disappear as quickly, to melt into the landscape, to adapt himself with this agility to changes in décor, temperature, and mood, it seemed to him that he would finally feel he belonged.

He trains every day. He can now leave the communal bubble without causing the slightest ripple. When he returns, several hours later, nobody thinks to ask him to account for himself. The Cluster is a latitudinarian municipality. Civility is its regime of stability, if he wasn't heard leaving, his return shouldn't be noted either. He nonetheless senses all the sidelong glances and the effort that some have to make in order not to contravene the rule. Rhif knows he will have made an enormous amount of progress when he is able to return as discreetly as he leaves. To be there, once again, among the others, as if he had never gone out. Being in two places at once is the octopus's knowledge. A gift directly correlated to that of continual transformation. Rhif may well know a number of animal ruses, the billions of forms of life in their four dimensions, the miraculous inventions of the abysses, he's enchanted by the octopus's fugitive qualities. Of course, it can ventilate with its siphon open and bolt like any old swift fish, but its running speed is its last resort. The escape inside its body is what captivates him. This way of sinking into ectoplasms, taking refuge there, overturning orders, kingdoms, and genera by cutting across all of them, as easily as swimming freestyle.

Observation is not the only key. Rhif has spent hundreds of hours in a kitted-out patrol. From a very young age, he's been watching the milieu in which he lives and for which the Old-Ancestors made so many offerings. He knows how to listen with his skin, using his sense of smell and his palate's taste buds to find his way in the wakes whose waves have died away. His vision is increased tenfold by the red mask. The webbing of his fingers is supple and well maintained. He is patient, able to lie in wait for a long time and to get going in the blink of an eye, he knows his weapons. He also knows his maps, the number of hiding places likely to welcome him, and the fundamentals of inter-species negotiation. But he does not know how to insert himself into all the places his head goes. And he has trouble tying together two contradictory movements.

When he rises to the Border, crossing through multiple stages of blue in a color chart stretching from steel to azure, he propels himself with beautiful efficiency. The totality of his anatomy participates in moving him forward, he knows how to coordinate his limbs, his deep muscles support him, he alternates between filling up and expressing at an optimal rhythm, and the effort flows into his path with ease. Until aquamarine, he's comfortable. He can stay there, in dorsal recumbency, given up to the current, confident, occupied with watching the play of shadows in the large stalks of the canopy or the whirlpools dug out by the agitation of the surface. Rhif is inclined to lengthily contemplate the articulation of the bubbles projected into the vegetation, the way they form muddled swarms that are suddenly soothed, the way they burst at the deepest point of their descent, and the avidity with which they climb back up. The frenetic shimmying of the largest ones, the hasty discretion of the smallest, the rigorous streams of the tiniest—he finds them all worthy of interest. He's sometimes asked himself if the ones that stick to the stalks, sacrificing half their volume, or that are under the sheets of kelp, clinging obstinately to their support, were trying to imitate limpets. If, at bottom, this apparently empty shell nonetheless contained something or if it was waiting, riveted to its trunk, for a hermit-crab with green eyes, less caparisoned still than itself, to choose it for its home.

Rhif is educated. He knows where he comes from, which maneuvers were made and repeated, over the course of how many generations, to get them to what they are. The Reefers' innate memory is complete. They acquire the rest—experience—from the unpredictable events that give rise to their birth and, with varying degrees of harshness, welcome them. He knows that the bubbles are inert. He's observed their instantaneous dilution upon contact with the surface. And he knows that, on the other side, the diluted bubbles form a layer as thick as the ocean, that mountains and arid plains are found there, that the black smokers have ceased their activity. Above all, he knows, unlike the majority of his acquaintances, who have never left the great bath, that he comes from this airy environment.

Rhif isn't looking to cross the Border for good, but he's been training to jump over for a long time. By following the dolphins' hunting trips or games, he's started copying their bucking and spinning twists. The drive is primordial—issued at the strongest point of an acceleration in a straight line, from the end of the tail, at the appropriate moment, it enables jumps several fathoms above the surface. The dolphins are experts with figures, Rhif has seen dozens of them carry out a somersault, then take off in the opposite direction with double the vigor. The whales are less fanciful, but when their mass punctures the ceiling, taking in the gas and splitting the swells, accompanied by all this captive effervescence, the lesson is prodigious. What he dreams of is a moment of rest, a kind of pause, really lasting in the leap.

For some time now, he's been going on more solitary treks. It's a behavior that's programmed into the Reefers, they leave the municipality when they reach maturity. Group excursions, breaks of several hours, then several days, are the harbingers of this definitive departure. The solo climb is the last phase of one's education.

Rhif is precocious. He doesn't voluntarily share his adventures and distrusts his siblings' stories. His peers were born at the same time as him, the Reefers are all contemporaries, from the same cluster, genetically close—with the same rights, in the same boat, they raise each other tapping into a shared sensory and mnemonic material. The Old-Ancestors had ordained that it be so during the first controlled diachronic modifications. The radical measure of programmed death after replication, unanimously adopted, was decisive for the safeguarding of specific old characteristics. Rhif doesn't doubt its appropriateness. In this way, intergenerational problems are solved before they arise. And each new formation, naïve, nonetheless made up of deep traces of its forebears, finds itself free to tackle the world however it wants. Nobody starts from zero. The Reefers are born liberated, equipped, and not very programmed, save for learning and for dying at the right moment.

Some sink in, some stay just beneath the surface, crepuscular, some rise. They have all the skills needed to traverse levels and settle wherever they want to.

The slowness of the abysses is a chosen way of life. At this altitude, the density of the fluid determines elementary physiological activities.

Respiration, swimming, manducation, the slightest thought are subjected to a phenomenal constriction. Resources are rare; energy, difficult to obtain, is expended with the greatest frugality. A bullhead shark thinks seriously before giving a single swing of its tail or executing a change in direction. The cycle is slow. The visions, fabulous. Solar power doesn't reach these great depths. The axle around which the world spins is buried, exclusively terrestrial. Magnetism is felt. Bodies are magnificent.

An abyssal Reefer never returns. Their abilities, their physique, their clock adapt as time goes by. Their reveries are thick, their encounters infinite. Their habits are meditative out of necessity. Their red mask becomes black, protuberant, their dimensions increase, their nose is infallible, and their hearing is synchronized with the horizontal sheet that covers the globe. They can hear, from the other end of the world, any sound emitted on their level. The sinking cadaver of a whale, the wheezing of a city of smokers and the pattering of the shrimp who feed there. When a worm leaves its tube and filtrates, when a sole gets stuck in the sand, when a crab seizes its prey, they pick up on it. They can situate an event in space and time—what they can't do, unless it's right in front of them, is join in. In the middle of all these data, their survival is uncertain.

Rhif has observed the octopuses in this section. They are magical. Unbearably fragile, in complete contradiction to the crushing conditions of life in the depths. Not much bigger than a closed fist, light, orange or blue when resting, their pupils rimmed with white, they wear their tentacles short, their fins like ears. Their large, full eyes soak up the darkness. Like their aphotic cousins, they borrow from a vast variety of identities with great agility. The tiny gray elephant set down on the deserted floor, wrinkly, older than the dawn of time, turns itself inside out like a glove lined with silk to make room for the sea anemone, delicate sensitive carnivore, soft enough to throw you into a fit of ecstasy. Rhif had touched several of them with the tip of his finger, each time receiving the baptism of skin-to-skin contact, the kiss of life.

Abyssal excursions are extreme. Pressure acts as an amplifier, reflexes are dreadfully fast, like lightning, the excessive poverty and richness of these waters is uncompromising, the combats more than mortal, the emotions, radical. Life is uncompromising close to the Earth's core.

The Reefers who make this choice are athletes and, in a way, Rhif admires them, but his personal penchant, no matter what he thinks about it, carries him to the Border. As if he were weighed down, more than others, by a floating past that doesn't commit to sinking completely.

He can't believe those who claim to find, so deep down, the best kind of security. He's seen too much in terms of volcanic eruptions and blind predation. The bioluminescent ballets that are constantly taking place, delighting his eyes and spirit, are just so many lures or warnings, enchanting defense mechanisms, but Rhif can't enjoy the spectacle while knowing that each luminous pulsation is, perhaps, the last one before being devoured. He cannot tolerate these contrasts.

The adherents of the middle life don't win him over either. They repeat so many questionable things about what might have taken place between the aphotic and photic zones, and, worse still, at the surface, that you'd need to be simple-minded to not make out the beginnings of an ideology in what they say. Even if the programming of the sinking instinct is reinforced through their acquired genes, this doesn't correspond to either an order or a recommendation. Rhif is convinced that its continued presence has the virtue of contradicting an instinct that is older and more anchored in the species, and of thus provoking, on the part of all the Reefers—whether they like it or not—the inevitable exercise of freedom. Upon reaching maturity, they will be obligated to choose. Nobody remains in the Cluster after the preliminaries.

He's been to confabulations where some of his peers, still half-larval, pride themselves on having a mental imagery that's complete with respect to mythical times. According to them, before the great Corrections, the Old-Ancestors dragged themselves about on the other side of the surface. They had tails divided in two all the way to the middle of the body and stood on these two shaky sections while trying to keep their head at the axis of the backbone. Their hands weren't webbed, their skin was rough, they wore algae above the eyes and on the forehead, their crotches were weirdly open or swollen, they were soft. Very weak, unfit for survival, they nevertheless clung to an exosomatic culture that was unimaginably large. Their Clusters were huge and covered most of the arid expanses. They never left them. Maturity did not reach them. Civility wasn't their shared political regime—they didn't have one. Their fragility was made up for by a proliferating fecundity; as is the case in all poorly armed species, they compensated for their losses through reproduction on a massive scale. When the losses diminished, they didn't take any measures. Before the formation of the Dust, the Clusters all touched each other, penetrated each other, until they were piled up on each other. The deserts were completely teeming with Old-Ancestors.

And then, since Zoï is the material of equilibrium, and one cannot persevere in existing, out of the wet, for the entirety of a specific life, the survivors made the decision to evolve.

Rhif accepts the past but when the stories touch upon what the half-larvae, who speak the moment the twilight reaches the middle waters, have supposedly seen, he reserves judgment.

For having ascended frequently to the kelp forest, he thinks of himself as having the right to doubt. It might be possible to swim in the thickness of the diluted bubbles while making do with a poor, unfiltered helioxygen, if done briefly. But that there might be life on the other side of the swells that can handle the void is unthinkable.

They speak of fish that are even more deformed still than the Old-Ancestors. Bodies whose heads are detached and hang from the end of a thick member, organisms whose fins have calcified, from which the scales have fallen off. They have huge square teeth and multiple, aberrant joints. There are flocks of them and they are frighteningly fast. Some say that you can sometimes hear rumbling through the surface and that it's these panicked animals taking flight. Rhif doesn't believe it. The rising tide stirs up the rocks and provokes anxiety-inducing acoustic invasions. The broken-coiled rhythms are destabilizing. Not once has a shadow projected itself above him at the Border when he was in the dorsal position, even though he has spent entire days there.

The stories didn't stand a chance of making him give up his training.

He improves his self-control day after day. He can hold on for ten minutes on the other side now.

He doesn't keep at a distance, he carefully spots his points of entry and never loses sight of possible egresses, he knows the coastline with increasing precision.

Up to five or six fathoms deep into the dry earth, there are only black rocks placed onto the sand. Algae grow there still, but atrophy on the spaced-out blocks. He removes his mask to look at the Border beyond the Border and sees a long line in the place of cubic capacity.

There are crabs. He studies them because they are experts, leaping from place to place to reach the green prairies that are inaccessible through natural passages. Rhif doesn't understand why they avoid the water holes where they could find their oxygen. Maybe they're poisoned. He would need to check, but he has no desire to draw from the puddle of stagnant water he's been looking at with a sense of disgust for some time now. It's murky. The sand is lightly agitated, although it isn't in contact with the ocean and the countercurrents are non-existent. It isn't logical. He gets close enough to brush up against it, then, all of a sudden, he understands. An octopus covers the bottom of the basin and twists and turns enough to make one believe the tide has returned. Rhif smiles at her. She's seen him. She opens a vertical eye and winks. She leaves her clothes behind on the sand and sends to him the colors of encounter. Alternating between ultramarine and fuchsia pink. She reaches out a tentacle to him, he approaches his hand, wrapping around it. She sniffs him, tastes him. Her suckers sting his skin, she's tickling him on purpose. If he tries to reciprocate her caresses, she will get scared, he's tried it out more than once. He doesn't move.

And, all of a sudden, as if she fancied him, she comes all the way out of her water hole and places her swollen head against his mask, touching his ears and mouth, deploying two other tentacles, she kisses him, two hundred suction pads are stuck to his face and move like a supple, sensual, confusing wave. Rhif is shaken. The octopus shows him her trust through her skin, through gentleness, insistence, then, suddenly, she detaches and clings onto the surrounding rocks, sliding, sticking, crawling, scaling, before tumbling down into a deep basin. Rhif needs to make a decision without waiting. Return to the Border, fill up well and come back, or imitate her. He imitates her. He doesn't need to think about it. He's loved octopuses for too long to resist this invitation she's extending to him. He plunges his head in with her and breathes. He hears her siphoning next to his ear. Their intimacy in such a reduced space is immediate. They know each other, they're sharing the source, they've got the world to themselves, populating it. The basin is an oasis, a bowl of hope in the aridity, an open promise. Then it's Rhif who changes color, turning pink. She replies to him by bristling with papillae, then, smooth once more, she takes him by the hand and leads him.

The water reserves in which she drags him get farther and farther away from the shoreline, and Rhif is happy to follow her, he feels guided, aspirated, appeased by the knowledge of these spaces that she displays and proves to him, step by step. He trusts her like he trusts himself.

At the end of the day, they find a deep pond, its water hardly salty at all. They've kept up their travel at a quick pace, without stopping, Rhif is satisfied, tired, groggy. He takes a rest. The octopus is on his belly. He sees the surface the way he would look at it from the ocean, lined, familiar and sparkling. Then a shadow alights. Doesn't pass, grows, gets bigger, covers the pool. Its form is soft, moving, it is enormous. The octopus hides behind his back. He feels her suckers, tense, clinging to his spine. The shadow rummages around the pool, it takes up all his attention. He doesn't feel the tentacles releasing their grip, escape escapes him, the water around him is bubbling, his mask fogs up, he is outside, held, prey to a set pressure, and he sees them—the enormous ones, the unthinkable cephalopods who have taken possession of the desert and hollowed it out.

The Kuīn

She is at the heart of the circle, the center of the square, without a stage, at the lowest point of this desert, eighteen meters in circumference, where nobody will join her.

Forms of display haven't changed much since the tragedies of antiquity.

She hasn't aged, she will not age. Her two braids, rolled up on themselves, are stuck to each side of her head. They protect her two brains and her cortex, her neck is bare, her occiput is very visible in the long-distance scope.

The screens lining the stadium both inside and outside show her coloring, the bridge of her nose, her closed mouth, the steadfast focus that has brought her this far, to today, to this place, intact, and less sure of herself than of her vision.

She isn't here to persuade, that time has long since passed.

The crowd is silent, attentive, aware of the physical dimensions of the site, of its relative mass. Their eyes are closed or wide open, riveted by the support polygon she places on the ground between her feet, all its threads drawn. They sparkle. The mental projections of the thousands of people present run along the length of the rays and move onto the centripetal spiral, whose magnitude is revealed bit by bit. The form extends well beyond the stadium, going past the reach of the speaker relays. Not everyone is there to listen.

Great Koré isn't waiting any longer. She holds herself upright, expressionless, barely denser than a hologram, solid like a fact. She's not asking anything of them, neither welcome nor attention, she lets them do whatever. Unload, send images and waves, the tensions stemming from the hope spots they're arriving from.

They've come in great numbers, almost all of them, except the infants and the wounded, from far away, very far indeed, and the fatigue from the journey subdues or accentuates what they broadcast according to their personality. She lets them be. Smooth, poised inside the penalty box with its cribellate centrifugal weave, which ensures an insulation worthy of a Faraday cage.

Great Koré presents no hand or toeholds, she's never done so. The representations glide around her, their feelings brush up against her, their passions evaporate before reaching her. Her physiognomy does not express affect. Her face's youthfulness and nakedness have functioned as defensive and offensive weapons, beyond any idea of mastery. Her detonation speed relies on this involuntary impermeability. She has little use for catalysts. If she had wanted to manipulate them, in one way or another, she would have failed.

The hope spots are violent spots, it couldn't be any other way. What reaches her through the rays and the curves is brutal, bloody, interwoven with predation. Thousands of consciousnesses expressing themselves on the web bear witness to violence, birth, the resistance and dislocation of bodies. Fission, fusion, cellular division, devoration and excretion, revolt.

The simulacra they transmit are tinged with judgment. Behind the apparent diversity of these spontaneous and painful manifestations, Great Koré feels the same, singular, eternal demand that one addresses only to a parent or to a god—relief. Which is, at bottom, be it a prayer or a demand, a misplaced petition.

She lets things slide.

She lets the void respond to the smoke.

The bonds come undone for lack of anything to stick onto.

They call her Kuīn, Koroleva, Amelka, Great Shimé for precisely this reason, that, at her feet, their pendants fall as they make them.

They come from cities and light up megalopolises, they come out of occupied schools, libraries, wildernesses, and forests, out of commandeered buildings. They come from new archipelagos, from restoration pockets that have burst. They come out of power plants, train stations, paralyzed airports, highways, gutted zoos.

They come from cities that have been taken over, where jaguars kill the dogs and children that wander at night, from coral reefs where the smallest eutrophic crack is fought over, where cans of food are refuges and weapons, they come out of riddled woods eaten away and fertilized by bat guano, they come from the sand deserts and the dust deserts that are swept through by tornados, they turn up out of thick seas, saturated with duckweed. They come from excess and the destitution it causes. They live there, they feed off it, they die from sickness, they know pleasure there, and a joy that is brief. They are young. They have followed her since the beginning. She is their Kuīn.

From her, one charters clean trains, hybrid sailboats, gentle and hardy mares, fast camels. She possesses nothing, the only thing that she doesn't part with is a backpack with a capacity of twenty liters, which contains a flexible wing and a reversible sleeping bag. When possible, she calculates her trips according to what winds, bubbles, and hills she can take off from. She travels light. She's gone wherever she hasn't been expected. This is her fourth trip around the world since planting herself in front of her village's parliament. Now, she's no longer alone, millions of people accompany her, waiting for and watching out for her, wherever she is and whatever she does, she is under the eyes and in the hearts of those she's lifted up and propelled into action and instant power. As untouchable as that first day and for the same reasons. Great Shimé has always accepted, always rejected the same things, in all possible worlds, without worrying about adapting. She has not matured. She could only disappear. The hair fluttering about her neck attests to this. She arrived whole, but has had to learn how to breathe. Despite her immutability, uncommon for a human being, the Kuīn is an organism, an open system whose door can slam shut.

In the eyepiece of the long-distance scope, the situation is simple.

The hope spots are tougher than they thought. The joy of overthrow is long behind them, behind her. This outburst of reactive energy triggered the first updates, it erupted in the streets and shook up institutions. The power in place, in all places, wavered. Backed up by the droughts, the tsunamis, the last black tides, the steppe fires, the volcanic eruptions coming out of the permafrost, the protestors shook out their old rugs through the windows, sometimes letting them fall.

When an animal devours its offspring, you take its litter away from it and kill the animal.

When a species multiplies without any regard for its possibilities of survival, it offers up its children to the environment, gives them over to rot, to reconstitute the humus it had worn out, making its descendants into the food for its unending feast. Tender bodies are quickly recycled. But young brains are malleable, quick, capable of producing gauze on top of a gaping wound, of making do without foundations, of suturing torn-out microconnections.

The facts don't force themselves. The facts are there. They're not visible as long as one doesn't see them.

In the same way she holds herself up in the center of the depression carved out by her corporeal mass in the silk web that carries her, in the position of being seen and taken into consideration, she held the world up before their eyes in the form of a globe of liquid glass where the biological, meteorological, seismic and migratory events that had indeed taken place on earth played out in miniature.

Over the course of solitary weeks, before her village's parliament, then before the parliaments of her country, of neighboring countries, of far-away countries, of unreachable countries, she contented herself with holding out, at arm's length, a subtle artifact connected to current scientific data. An elegant miniature, animated by shades of color and somersaults, an object that leapt in her hand when it took in the large tremors, the synoptic frictions and storms.

Because it was small enough to make one want to be careful with it, they saw it. Because there were a lot of them, more and more of them to take note of it, they accepted to see what they saw. And to take the material of their future into their hands, along with burning smoke.

Now, her palms are empty. She, the Kuīn, is the only one standing at the middle of the web where the pearls have finished oozing. The silks are dry. Hearts have expressed themselves, drop by drop, she is not the site of their complaint. She isn't responsible for anything. They didn't elect her, she showed up, she was there.

She began to speak at the beginning of her

second journey around the world, when the ball of liquid glass, fissured at the poles and at the pacific ridges, had become too fragile to be manipulated. When the adults' clothes started to shrink and let doubt emerge, started to show their skinny legs, their useless arms, their thick necks. When the powerful among them appeared on the screens as they were: in gatherings, capitular meetings around the world, out of breath, strangled by their neckties and ribbons, hampered by their shoes, covered with prostheses. Incompetent.

She spoke to say what she saw. That she accepted seeing what she saw, that she was proof of it. And everyone saw it then with her, the emperor's clothes were far from new, they weren't beautiful, or sumptuous, but they didn't reek either, they weren't simply unstitched or torn off by dogs—the king, before these finally open eyes, was naked. The king had disappeared. With him, trust, their guide, their recourse, the possibility of legitimate hate, of a court, of obedience, of sleep.

The powerful among the grown-ups, or those who wanted to be, did what they could to cover themselves. They pled. They assuaged. They looked down on others, cracked jokes, and continued to put their asses, balls, pussies, and elbows onto the ornamental, waxed furniture of their plenary meetings. Without seeing each other, without seeing themselves. Naked as they were, squeezed in tight, they didn't feel the air move. They didn't understand that it was blowing in from the ice floes and the forests at the same time, that it was gathering its strength above the continents that it would sweep through, kicking up lots of dust. They hadn't seen the shot go off. The butterflies disappearing with their biographers they had no use for, the dogs getting larger, the viruses teeming in the ever-shrinking pie, the earth's mangy crust, drilled even in its deepest wrinkles. The sand that had been transformed into cement, the beaches into landslides, the waters into mercury, the grasshoppers into vessels. They refused to see what they saw. The young girl with the smooth skin who, too calm, held out the world to them as it was, a mirror in which they could have recognized themselves and touched their wounds the way the great apes and wild elephants do.

She came out of nowhere. She fell from the sky, hang-gliding smack dab into the middle of their great council without any warning, she remained silent in the assembly room until camera lenses and the phones' ears picked her up. They took selfies and author photos at her side. Showing off their size and the elegant costumes of an extinct world. The Kuīn was a block, a pioneer with no hat or visor, her squasachim braid contained in her crossed arms. Out of which one couldn't get anything. The smiles were wiped off their faces, seriousness took over. Then condescension, reprimands, attempts at intimidation, threats. And during this time when they could have put their fingers on their open wounds and begun to heal something, to take out the knife, nine-year-old kids led airstrikes with their video game controllers, odd ten-year-olds manipulated gene scissors in their parents' garages, intersex people of the same age bred cultivars in abandoned greenhouses. Honey harvesters that were 120 centimeters tall fabricated climbing insects, non-binary Ethiopians developed brigades of self-driving anti-mine bushes and cleaned up militarized lands. The average age of hackers reached a peak of twelve years old. Running away increased at a rate never before seen.

Groups formed spontaneously. The coordinates of islets dedicated to voluntary formations began to circulate in the network reserved for the under fifteen crowd. The interface proposed general thematic choices and, based off their point of departure, oriented them toward the nearest junctions. Critters, Comput, Stars, Wargame, Horror were some of the most popular domains. Wild camps propagated as well, outside of any physical or virtual cartography. One came into being as soon as three children got together for several hours or for months, weeks, on land gone to waste, in a corner of the forest, a cave, an abandoned studio or factory. They lived, slept, played, ate whatever together. They taught themselves to cross rivers, to go down highways the wrong way, to fool police cordons. They developed a heightened awareness of corridors and clandestine resources. They switched between specialties. A Critter could transmit their experience with animal silks or what they knew about sericogenic glands to a Chemik and a Techno could seize the information needed for taking on the fab of a digital prosthesis. They knew their classics. They were chock-full of an unverified encyclopedic knowledge and heaps of tutorials since birth. Nobody made them take baths, move in bipedal fashion, eat carrots. They could caulk their huts with cob made from their waste if they so pleased.

During her third trip around the world, Great Shimé had visited model islands. The Critters of the Amazon who had replaced spoken language with sign language to include young monkeys and *runa puma* jaguars in everyday debates. The Critters of Siberia, out in the middle of nowhere, where the felt habitat was divided horizontally. She held onto a warm memory of a night, snowy at last, when the Tribe had invited her to sleep in the pile of Samoyed dogs and quilts of goose down. They were staunch caninemen, everyone there knew how to turn off a faucet with their teeth, put down their head to greet one another, move their ears independently. She had watched the dog-man pack circle the Orlov trotters on the steppe at daybreak and the sounds of the race had resonated through her hood like an ebbing tide.

She had flown in the company of the Polatouchs of Norway, along the Troll Wall and above the fjords. These Nordic gliders had modeled their wingsuits after the flying squirrels of Africa. They were fur-lined, white underneath, and tagged with acrylic on the back. From the takeoff point, one could tell them apart from each other up until they deployed their landing parachutes. During her visit, the entire troupe had jumped with her. Halfway down the cliff face, she saw herself surrounded then passed by a cloud of little bodies with their short wings wide open. They buzzed as they fell and she had the furtive feeling of being a queen bee attached to a heavy mushroom, escorted by her vibrating swarm and in search of a new hive.

She had chatted for a whole night in a club for black-toothed fairies conducting research on using carbon nanotube sensors to decontaminate the water flowing from their ceiling.

Several Bunks had welcomed her into their self-governed caves, natural and made of concrete, and shown her the locations of similar structures throughout the entire world. Hundreds of them.

Several Farms had shown her their cabins on every continent. She had seen fields on bales of straw, green roofs, walls covered with vegetables, huge geodes held up by lignified tendrils. In industrial wastelands, elevated parking garages, on tarmacs, in suburban zones—everywhere asphalt was cracking—they threw things to grow that grew. Everywhere in the forest or what remained of it.

She was familiar with the Graphs' physical shelters and their 3D and laser printer facilities. Visual art spread in the streets, on murals or installed by six-year-old billposters having a grand time with their glue-filled pails and giant brushes slung around their shoulders. In Europe's cities, there was no longer a single grown-up around to make unwelcome comments to a six- or eight-year-old little person. One's pail could drip all along the length of a subway station, or stain passersby, people turned their heads to look elsewhere.

In the United States, the elderly stocked up on provisions and barricaded themselves in their homes during Halloween. In Manitoba, grown-ups no longer opened their doors ever since a phalanx of Critters had made their candy run under the supervision of a polar bear. It took a week after

the holiday to rid the trees of their toilet paper gar-
lands and to collect the trash cans that had been
burnt to a crisp.

In the summer, racetracks popped up in the
countryside. Stretches of roads and highways were
converted and blocked off by hay bales. Crash bar-
riers were removed when they got in the way of
the route. The competitors took off at full speed at
the signal, all categories combined—kart, buggy,
customized tractor, Ferrari, or roll cages—as long
as it had a motor and four wheels, a vehicle was
approved. The oldest pilots had learned to drive
on Crazy Taxi or Mario Kart, low blows were par
for the course and participants didn't take off without a bag of banana skins, paint bombs, and tire
knives. Engines ran indiscriminately on canola,
ethanol, ammoniac, or algae—the atmosphere
was thick. In Auckland, Great Koré had inaugu-
rated the first contest for carts propelled entirely
by liquid hydrogen before going to Japan for the
spring cosplay convention, where everything fell
apart.

The cosmopolitan cream of the crop among
the Geeks, who were responsible for the phantom

network's relays, had put out the idea of an inter-national *kosupure* meet. Different experiments with flash physical actions had been carried out successfully a few months prior. In a blitz, King-Fahd's soccer stadium in Riyadh had, during the quarterfinals of the new Cup of confederations, been turned over to two ultimate frisbee teams, Colombia's under-sixteens and the Dubliners.

Skateboarders in the six-to-eight-years-old group had discovered spots inside London, Hong Kong, and Frankfurt's stock exchanges. They had invaded the spaces of finance for a night of boarding—gloved, helmeted, masked, armed with compact cruisers and an impressive mastery of London Gaps and slides. They pumped hard, rode quickly, and had a ball in the rotundas and on the ramps. The new, super-minor special response teams had taken three hours on average to drive them out. In the time that they kettled them out-side, journalists were on site and citizen cameras were capturing their slightest movements.

Other types of events, intentionally on a smaller scale, were taking place on each continent, serving as tests. Reactivity was optimal, and the twenty-and-overs were beginning to notice it and become alarmed.

When Great Shimé had arrived in Tokyo, the Harajuku and Shibuya neighborhoods had been cordoned off. One could not pass. The Tokyo Dome was surrounded by soldiers in tactical gear two rows deep. At the same time as the others, she received the redirection notifications and the transportation instructions. Thousands of phones beeped in unison, kicking off the show.

The cosplayers set off from the outskirts of their designated neighborhoods, now suddenly blocked off, as well as from the Dome around which they had gathered. They walked side by side in their grand festive attire, filling the avenues, blocking the intersections, sidewalks, and bus lanes. They flowed through the streets like a flood, infiltrating the subway tunnels. In twenty minutes, one of Tokyo's hearts was stopped, stunned by the surge of costumes and animal energy going around. They headed toward the train station. In three-piece suits, short skirts, suits or veils, passersby were swept up by the wave—immediately caught up, they melted into the mass and marched with it.

The officers succeeded fairly quickly in determining the demonstrators' objective and the movements of the group converged toward Haneda airport and the Chidoya district.

Suidobashi Nishidori Avenue's three kilometers were swallowed up by an uninterrupted wave from the bridge in front of the Dome to the Takebashi subway station. The cosplayers wanted to pass Hirakawamon Gate and enter Chidoya through the park, but the special forces were stationed on the peninsula, Fujimi Temple behind them, Kikyō-mon Gate on their right, closed off by three armored vehicles ready to contain those arriving in the narrow perimeter of the East gardens.

While the front line forced its way through at Takebashi, the rearguard continued to parade in front of Kanda University's campus, overjoyed. The Akira and Astroboys had come to the front of the procession, supported on the sides by the great Zatoïchi swordsmen and Champloo samurais in tight formation. Several dozen rusty strollers squeaked in front of the fake blind people heading straight for the Tenjin-bori Moat with the intention of bypassing them on their left. Blocked by the police, who were beginning to retreat from the driving force of the Terminator, Transformer, and Replicant super-armed giant robots, the sighted blind forded the water in one go.

In groups of twelve, the full set of Avengers followed the sweet and gothic Lolitas who were following the samurais. Flanked by several Dr Manhattans decked out in a wide range of blues, and by clone Stormtrooper soldiers, they spilled over to the east and west of the moat onto drenched grass.

Zombies from *The Walking Dead*, Gandalfs, vampires from *True Blood*, old-school Draculas, Evilmans, and a good number of Maids and Decora Kei supported the advance toward the buildings of the Museum of the Imperial Collections, heavily guarded by armed men who couldn't believe their eyes. Rorschachs circulated among the factions, perhaps with a watchword.

Spidermen leapt onto the steps tossing streamers about that stuck to the clear shields. Links fired arrows in every direction. A red Spock and a blue Spock tried to keep clear of the overheated Jokers, but when the group at the tail end appeared, with Hulk at the front, very green, very irritated, surrounded by several bloody clowns from *It*, their hands full of multicolor balls, and when they were joined by Yondu, Yoda, and the black spirit from *Spirited Away*, the cooker was on the verge of exploding.

There was a lull of two seconds, two miraculous seconds, then all it took was one Demogorgon, from on top its stilts, rising up on its hind legs and half-closing the carnivorous flower of its head around that of a frontline police officer, for the war to break out. It was dazzling.

The pirates from *One Piece* threw themselves at the legs of the first-comers, swords between their teeth. The billy clubs came off the belts in one fell swoop and began to churn the air in front of them. The angels and the Morningstars deployed their large shield wings and beat the air to give the Supers time to intervene. Luffy and the other Elastics tried to throw the ranks off balance by launching flexible arms and legs to kneecap them from behind. This tumbling down had notable effects on the median barrier, the police got back up in disarray, their hands full of grenades. At the sight of this, the Kawaiis entered the fray, opening their big kitty eyes and, screaming, took to clawing at their pants. Joined by zombies, some of whom were really bleeding, and by a group of old Smurfs led by a raging Snow White and six Daeneryses, mothers of dragons, in equestrian leather, the front line was knocked down by this latest go. The aerosols whizzed, whistling, toward the lawns, and brought the Astros, samurais, and bots back into the heart of the fray. There was total confusion and the outcome was uncertain until the Batmans, Bayonettas, Shazams, raring-to-go Jean Greys, Supers, Irons, Wonders, Marios and Luigis, and flying Harrys let themselves drop from the rooftops onto which they had climbed. The blow that was dealt, a terrific collective combo more radical than Rashid's Altair, was fatal to the police.

The three armored vehicles' water cannons only served to clarify the situation. The cosplayers' weapons warped, but the authorities were on the ground. Stunned.

You know the rest.

The takeover of Shinkansen, the triumphant arrival at Nagoya, two weeks of a mind-blowing International, and the ultimatum addressed to the politicians and multinationals at the conclusion of the longest minor-citizen debate ever held.

Then the grown-ups' lie. The lie repeated over and over again. And Great Shimé's absolute determination at the most confusing moments.

Once again, she was there, six months after the events and the extreme repression, in plain sight. Alone at the center of the penalty box, her skull protected by two braids rolled up on themselves, her forehead bare. Pale, poised. The mental projections of the thousands of children gathered around her had dripped down to her feet and come undone there. She was going to speak.

She was going to tell them there will be no life

What is called
        If we consent to exhibit ourselves under
              the bots' sensors
        If we leave the Earth behind like an aban-
              doned playground

If we can witness the collapse of birds and
   not go mad
If we take up our pail and shovel once
   more to excavate in wells
If we are satisfied with being bones with-
   out flesh, husks without seeds
Life
   Without taking the monkeys—and the
      fools—as our thought masters
   Without plunging into plants, hands
      clasped out front
   Without inventing horses and dogs
   Without leaving it to the slowest of planti-
      grades to hold the world up
   Without sinking into the ocean to, per-
      haps, be reborn there
There will not be any of it
For us

What if!

She breathes in, opening her mouth.
In the sights of the long-distance scope, her hair
flutters about her neck.

Acknowledgments

I would like to thank Céline Minard for entrusting me with the translation of this remarkable and strange text that is the future excavated from our past, and for her willingness to respond to all my questions, big and small. My thanks also to Léa Cuenin and Hannah Frydman for their careful, meticulous reading, and to Hannah in particular for cracking the text open like a recalcitrant pistachio in the moments I needed the most help. And thank you, Jeffrey Zuckerman, for cheering me along and sharing your wisdom with me.

The Author

After receiving her degree in philosophy, **Céline Minard** was a bookseller in Paris for seven years. In each of her books, she tries to explore new fictional territory, conducting vital experiences with times, places, voices, and bodies, in order to transcend literary forms. She is the author of several novels including *Le Dernier Monde* (2007), *Bastard Battle* (2008), and *So long, Luise* (2011). Her books have been translated into multiple languages.

The Translator

Annabel L. Kim is Professor of Romance Languages and Literatures at Harvard University and the author of two books: *Unbecoming Language: Anti-Identitarian French Feminist Fictions* (2018) and *Cacaphonies: The Excremental Canon of French Literature* (2022).

Printed in the USA
CPSIA information can be obtained
at www.ICGtesting.com
JSHW011457160924
69913JS00007B/13